They froze at the rustling sound of approaching footsteps in the hall behind them. A doorknob turned, followed by the squeak of hinges.

"Ciao," the woman said, gliding into view.

She stood with marvelous posture, wearing a long, skin-tight black dress and a black hat that was tall and pointed with a wide brim. Arnold shook like he was riding a boxcar. The woman's lips bunched in a half-restrained smile.

"My goodness," she said. "You have fear? You are wise to have fear."

She pivoted Arnold's table so that he was facing Wright. Wright remained stone-faced.

"Look at this one," the woman said, pointing to Wright. "Is soldier. Big, tough soldier man. Who do you call him? Mister Wright?"

Arnold nodded yes.

She sighed deeply as she walked in between the two tables. Wright turned to her.

"What are you?" Wright asked sternly, looking her up and down from the point of her hat to the hem of her dress. "You look like a witch."

She leaned in closer. "I show you what I am."

MALOCCHIO

Dark Magic of the Evil Eye

by

NICHOLAS ANTHONY

Malocchio
By Nicholas Anthony
Copyright © 2019 by Nicholas Anthony
All Rights Reserved.
Cover Design and Art by Henriette Boldt.
Interior Design and Layout by Rachel Reiss.
Developed and Edited by Stephen Parolini.
Edited by Michael Hals.
Published by RedLine Electronics, LLC.

Printed Book ISBN-13: 978-0-578-55617-8

Dear Reader, your thoughts and feedback are welcome in this creative landscape. It matters not what you think, it matters that you share it. Please, share a review.

Please go to ByNicholasAnthony.com *and Share a Review*

This tale was brought to fruition with the love and support of Mrs. Sharon Summers and Dr. Margaret Curtis, who each nurtured the creative process and provided deep and insightful support at critical intervals along the perilous journey. Thank you so much for dedicating your time, providing much-needed encouragement, and giving attention to detail.

Nicholas Anthony

Contents

MALOCCHIO

CHAPTER 1

Riding in the Jeep

THE JEEP'S MOTOR ROARED AS it sped along the beaten road, scattering flocks of scavenger birds that had landed to feast upon the dead dogs. Dark mounds of flesh spotted the military highways of northern Italy, lumpy and misshapen like rotten vegetables. In the last light of day, the piles cast shadows that looked like streaks of blood, as if the corpses had been thrown and made to skid violently before coming to rest.

Corporal Clyde Wright swerved to hit the bloated bodies, which had been swelling in the summer heat. It was now mid-summer, and the Americans had arrived in late March. Only four G.I.'s rode in the vehicle, and the lack of weight gave the jeep a loose maneuverability, a treat for the driver. The engine roared with freedom under Wright's heavy foot.

The dead were dogs of an Italian breed called the *corso*, aptly described by newly-promoted Private

First Class Samson Arnold as bricks with legs. By their numbers, it seemed the Italians were fond of keeping them as pets. Private First Class Jay Oaks pointed out the crater to the south.

"Nazi rubber plant," he laughed. He cupped his hand to his mouth and leaned out the side. "Hey, Hitler! The bombs are supposed to *bounce* off!"

Private First Class Edward Layne rode in the back. He knew Germans had never worked at that factory. It had been mostly Italians and Slavs, women and children, laboring against their will. Most American soldiers didn't know that. His companions continued laughing.

Wright and Oaks had promised Arnold, against the man's insistence, a night of drinks and whores to celebrate his promotion. Layne had been assigned to their patrol quad by chance. The 'patrol' first took them to the only pub, *La Terra Grandisima*, that was still open and wet in war-torn Ferarra, and now it took them driving out into the countryside.

The land around them was flat with deep irrigation ditches that ran parallel with the roads. To Edward it felt like they were always going uphill, and he could hear it in the jeep's motor.

"Fifteen minutes north," Oaks read from a crumpled paper. "Left at the crossroads with the roundabout, then about a mile." He kissed the paper. "Bless you, Signor Giaccomo."

"Yeah, sure," said Arnold. His forehead was slick with sweat despite the cool evening. With each of Arnold's words, his right eye gave a violent wink. He told everyone it was a reflex he'd developed as a kid that resurfaced after the landing. "God bless Giaccomo. Christ himself must have commanded the old-timer to give us directions straight to the border of Allied control. Hell, right now we're practically deserters! Promotion to dishonorable discharge, all in one week! So, *salute*! Mysterious fucking old man!" He held up his chubby hand in a mock toast.

"Quiet down, Private First Class Twitch," Wright called back.

Oaks ignored Arnold. "Hey Wright," Oaks said to the driver. "You think any of these gals speak American?"

Wright looked back at him. "Hell, I hope not. I ain't interested in any more conversation than I already got."

"I just want to hear that pretty girl-talk again. Damn, like the way them Alabama girls do it."

"You've been deployed for three months," Layne cut in.

"So what," Oaks said. "Ain't like I want to be here. If I had it my way, I'd be at the drive-in with one of my gals right now. 'Stead, I'm here with y'all."

"And next you'll be on your knees with Sargent Reynolds holding a gun to the back of your deserter head," Arnold said between tics. "We shouldn't be out here. They'll know we ain't on patrol."

"Just for that," Wright called back. "You get all the fat, twitchy ones."

"Now wait just a minute," Oaks said. "Some of us here prefer a portly gal. And they're hard to come by nowadays."

Arnold looked up from wiping his sweat-smeared glasses, wrinkled his nose and twitched. "You like 'em big?"

Oaks turned in the passenger seat to look back at Arnold. "I didn't," he said. "Not until your mother showed me the time of my life last night. Bless the big gals, alleluia amen!"

Arnold cursed and tossed a glove up at Oaks, but all three laughed and even Ed Layne cracked a smile.

"Anyways," Wright said. "If they're gonna court-martial us, they're gonna have to court-martial a hell of a lot of others." He pointed to the road ahead. "Look."

In the last remaining light of day they could see silhouettes of soldiers. As the jeep slowed, they saw a farmhouse set an eighth of a mile off the road, atop a gentle grassy hill. Wright brought the truck to idle where the path to the house began. More than a dozen soldiers stood stiffly, surrounding the house. Others lined the path to the porch like dominoes. Five paces separated each soldier from his counterpart. Each man stood at full attention.

The third story windows of the farmhouse shone brightly in the dusk, causing dark shadows to cover the faces of the soldiers. In the growing darkness, the windows of the farmhouse dominated the landscape like two giant eyeballs, surveying the new arrivals.

"Who they fightin' for?" Oaks asked no one in particular.

Wright looked thoughtful for a moment, and then he reached over and grabbed a fistful of Oaks' uniform. "This is good," he said. "The place has guards! What do you think them guards are guardin'?"

A smile widened Oaks' face. "Poo-tang."

"Yeah, buddy!" Wright slapped Oaks' chest then turned and jumped out of the truck. "My man Giaccomo tells no lies!" Oaks quickly followed. Despite his previous protests, Arnold gave a heft, then a leap, and his boots hit the ground with a thud.

"Whoa, slow down," Wright said as he walked around the truck. "Somebody's got to stay with the jeep." He took off his .45, his M1, and his knife and set them on the passenger seat. "And the guns."

"Shit, not me," Oaks said. He quickly began to disarm.

Arnold looked to Ed Layne, who had not moved from his seat in the truck.

"Well," Arnold said after a twitch. "Do you wanna-?"

"You go ahead, Private. It's your night." Ed grinned. "I'll stand watch."

Arnold relented, giving a close-lipped smile. "Thanks, Layne. I really don't want to piss off Reynolds, but-" he looked over his shoulder. "B-but I've really been thinking about... you know-"

"I know," Ed said. "Make it worth your lira."

Arnold smiled and winked at Ed. Then Ed realized it was just his twitch.

The three cohorts sauntered toward the house, laughing and joking as they passed by the silent guards. Ed moved Wright's weapons and took the passenger seat for himself. After digging through his pack a moment, he brought out Elizabeth's photo. It was from their college newspaper, *The Student Observer*. She had been the editor and Ed, as an excuse to talk to the smart and pretty girl from the journalism department, had submitted a few poorly written articles. Once he had heard her say that the photo he now held was the only one she liked of herself. He smiled, thinking about how pretty she looked in all her photos, and how insecure she felt about them. She had hated every picture the photographer took of her for the biography page. She always had mischief in her eyes, along with a grin that was only recognizable as a grin because the very corners of her mouth angled up just so. Once, Ed had asked her what she was thinking about when she made that face and she said "Strangling the cameraman, Ed. Strangling him to death." Ed sighed and looked up from her picture at the farmhouse and its two glowing eyes watching him, now all the brighter since dusk had turned to night.

CHAPTER 2

The Blood of Kings

A FEW MONTHS AGO, WHILE ON a march through a swampy area of southern France, Ed thought for the first time that he was going to die. A prone gunman had concealed himself in the brush, flanking Ed's left. Time froze when Ed noticed the gunman. His arms felt like they were tied with weights, and his fingers fumbled feebly at his weapon. The German's barrel fixed directly at his chest numbed Ed's ability to respond. His subconscious leapt into control at that would-be final moment of life and delivered him a memory of Beth so vivid it was as if all movement on earth had stopped. Ed never got a shot off, but he did not need to. If that gunman had been alive and not weeks dead, Beth would have been the last thing he thought of in this world. Not his mother, his childhood friends from back home, or even himself. It was all he could do not to jump up and down at the realization, there on the

edge of some low French swamp, boots muddy and pants soaked
from the bottom up, with a decaying man for an audience. Later,
he proceeded to write Beth a letter when they'd made port, but of
course he had no way of knowing if she'd gotten it.

The men were not surprised at Ed's whorehouse reluctance.
Most likely they'd planned on it. Back at base he was thought of
as dull, but officers had taken notice of his diligence and considered him to be at the start of a fine military career.

For an hour Ed thought of Beth's blond locks, the way they
sat on her shoulders and flowed down her back, while he wiped
his knife and guns. Then he grabbed another rifle and worked
on cleaning that. When he started on yet another, he glanced at
his watch and realized how many hours had passed. Although
the night was pitch-black in the surrounding countryside, the
light from those imposing farmhouse windows was enough for
him to work. He worked until he'd cleaned all their weapons,
even the Imperial pocketknife Oaks had looted from a dead
Germ, inscribed with the family name Gewählt. Arnold was
considered to be paranoid, but his point was gaining validity;
Sargent Reynolds would soon notice his missing patrol.

It was after another half hour of serious consideration that
Ed jumped off the truck and walked toward the first guard on
the path.

"Hey, good buddy," Ed said. "Speak the English?"

The guard said nothing. Ed was prepared to accept the possibility that he was speaking to a statue until he saw the man
breathe. Ed dared to lean in closer, trying to glimpse the man's
eyes. He couldn't see them. The green helmet, a standard issue of
sorts for any number of European foot-soldiers, sat low enough
on his head so that the eyes were lost in the night's heavy shadow.

"Parla l'italiani?" Ed tried clumsily.

Again, nothing.

The rifle that the guard held readied in his hand was an M1
Carbine, American issued, but the European had plenty of

them now, too. It was the sidearm that worried him. A Luger, German issued. An American would take a pistol like that for a trophy, but the Europeans that were still fighting hated everything German. And Ed was sure this guard wasn't American.

"Hey buddy. You talk? Hello?" He raised his voice, looking to the other soldiers standing about. "Anybody?"

Wind blew waves in the grass. Somewhere in the distance, an owl screeched. Ed huffed and began to walk to the house. A hot, prickly feeling started at his ears and worked its way down his neck. He cursed under his breath for not looking at the guards more closely upon arrival. High-priced whores, the old man Giaccomo had said. Some escapees from Rome before it was bombed. It made sense they'd be guarded, simply from a business standpoint. But as Sergeant Reynolds had often said: "The sooner you forget you're at war, the sooner you're reminded."

Ed's boots creaked on the floorboards as he walked onto the shadowed porch. Two guards stood protectively on either side of the door, though they made no move to stop him. The knob was coarse with rust but felt surprisingly sturdy. He turned it, pushed, and the door opened with ease. Ed walked into a room unlike anything he could have imagined.

It was immaculate, lavish, and muffled in silence. A bright Oriental rug covered the floor before him. Red and yellow drew his gaze. His eye followed a double medallion motif around the rug's border. Ironwood panels glowed with warmth from the walls, beautifully rendered with gold trimmed oak at the edges. Empty couches and chairs upholstered in blood-red velvet were placed alongside a massive white marble table at the center of the room. To move it must have required the strength of a dozen men. The pleasant smell of lilac suddenly yielded to an undertone of something burnt.

Ed gave a small start. Impressive though the room was, his gaze passed from it the moment the dark-haired woman appeared before him. She seemed to have been waiting for his notice. Ed must have stood in the doorway for too long, because she motioned with a ripple of her fingers for him to come in.

He obliged, closing the door behind him, trying to remember himself. The rug he stepped onto was so soft he could feel it through his boots. He immediately stepped back, afraid to track in dirt from outside. The woman laughed, girlish but soft and polite.

"Boots okay," she said with a heavy accent. "You are American. Yes. Good for you I speak so fine."

"Yes, hello ma'am," Ed said, suddenly embarrassed for a reason he did not know. "I am just here to-"

"To look for *i toui compagni*? Your friends?" She walked closer. The room was immaculate and his eyes wanted to take it all in, but the woman's presence demanded his full attention. Her long black dress left no doubt as to the perfection of her figure. It was cinched tight at her throat and covered the contours of her form entirely, leaving only the skin on her hands, neck, and face exposed. A mass of long, dark hair framed her pale cheeks and emphasized the startling brightness of her green eyes. She smiled. "I see you stayed in auto. *Forse...* you change mind?"

"No, ma'am," he said. "We're on a schedule, is all. Just need to collect the boys."

Her lips parted as her smile grew, showing the perfect white of her teeth. *A hungry looking mouth,* Ed mused, but the thought made him feel uncomfortable and he pushed it away.

"*Sempre la stessa...* boys always have difficulty to leave here," she said. Her voice was whimsical, like blowing the perfect note on one of those clay flutes the locals made in Sicily. "My name is Inara. I will call for your men. I cannot say no to handsome American boy."

He blushed a bit as she walked off. "My name's Edward Layne," he said. "Ed, really. It's short for Edward. You can call me Ed. Pleasure to meet you."

Inara stopped and turned. She looked down at his boots and, slowly, worked her gaze up his body until Ed felt a swooping leap in his stomach when her eyes met his own.

"We shall see. You have hunger?"

"No, not at all. But thank you."

"No, no, *grazie a ti.*" She turned again. "Please, come. You take *vino?* Eh . . . *wine?*"

Ed tried to answer, but found he could not. He was looking at her hair, flowing like ink suspended on her narrow back and pushing its tide down the widening beach of her hips. She walked with a poise that increased with each of her soft, soundless steps. The open area of the room led into a dark kitchen that was bordered by fine white countertops of marble, a wooden table in the center. The exotic rugs ended, and Ed's boots thumped against the polished hardwood. Inara's steps remained quiet.

An unlabeled bottle stood alone on the table. The woman strode over to it and Ed noticed how the bottom of her dress slid over the hardwood like liquid, yet curled at the end like the burnt page of a book. Behind her stood a gas stove, and in the corner was an ice chest. Finely-grained wooden cabinets with shiny brass handles lined the walls above the marble counters.

"May I get the cork for you, ma'am?" Ed heard himself ask. A glass of wine sounded very good to him just then. He deserved a slight luxury, given the kinds of fun the other three men were enjoying at the moment. Yes, enjoying a glass of wine with a beautiful woman would be fine enough indeed for Edward Layne.

Inara glanced over her shoulder. "You are sweet boy," she said with a soft smirk. "Very gentleman. Fetch a glass? *Per il vino?*" She gestured with her chin to the counter behind him.

He returned her smile and went to the task. The glasses were arranged on a circular wooden display, a small groove cut out for each individual stem, from which Ed carefully plucked two. He gave one to Inara, noting that the cork now rested neatly beside the wine bottle. Ed was just about to comment on her quickness when a loud noise and a bite of pain made him jerk. He looked down to see the shattered remains of the wineglass pinched between his thumb and middle finger.

"Oh no!" Inara said as she rushed over and seized his wrist. A sudden wave of dizziness washed over Ed. Blood arced out of the wound with each beat of Ed's heart. Delicately, she took his hand in hers and her white skin was sprayed with red. She trembled as she led him to the sink. His legs felt like they'd melted, but he went with her. His vision swayed in every direction. Bright roses blossomed upon the marble.

"Come," she whispered. "To the water."

Ed tried to laugh, tried to make a joke about the way Americans treat their hosts' glassware, but putting thoughts to words had become difficult. Looking over his shoulder at the blood trailed on the hardwood floor, a wave of vertigo took him. The feeling turned his stomach before it rose to the spot behind his eyes, where it blurred his vision.

"Blood loss," he managed to murmur. "Need to…put pressure."

They were over the water basin now. Inara guided his hand, held it under the spout, and turned the water valve, leaving a bloody fingerprint on the polished metal. The frigid water made the pain come alive. The sharp sensation brought Ed back to himself and his vision regained clarity. He saw the deep slice down the inside of his right middle finger.

Ed's training returned to him, and he pinched the injured finger with his left hand. He had already lost enough blood to feel faint, but any preemptive action was better than none. He saw a dish towel dangling at the edge of the porcelain basin, and he wrapped it tightly around his finger and applied as much pressure as he could. In what seemed like seconds, the white towel was saturated in red.

"Another towel perhaps, ma'am? Damnit, I'm going to need stitches." *And a cover story when I report to the infirmary.* Sargent Reynolds' disapproving scowl flashed in Ed's mind.

He continued to put pressure on his finger, leaning his weight on it between his good hand and the basin's edge. Pink water sloshed and gulped as it swirled down the drain.

"Ma'am?" he said, when the woman didn't reply. "Inara? I need another towel. Or a bandage. Ma'am?"

Ed looked over his shoulder, careful to keep his hand over the basin. Blood had soaked the towel and was dripping again. He turned the other way, where the kitchen led into a carpeted hallway. There was Inara, hunched over in the most curious position.

The blood that had speckled her hand moments before was gone. Now there was just bare white skin. She lapped at the webbing between her thumb and forefinger, oblivious to all else, like a kitten at a fresh saucer of cream.

When their eyes met, she pulled her hand from her mouth and froze. Her eyes burned green flames, but her brow was furrowed in worry, lips parted in shock as if they held one continual note. Chest heaving with increasing breaths, she reached backward to the counter for balance. Ed realized that he had come considerably closer to Inara without even noticing. He could feel heat radiate from her in waves with each of her deep breaths. A voice in his mind insisted that he should be repulsed by what she did, a woman who drank a stranger's blood, but there was a magnetic tug coming from her body.

The sleek curves apparent under her dress interested him greatly, but...but *Beth*. Beth had all that, and more. *Beth*, he thought, *my darling Beth. The dead gunman in France. Strangling the cameraman.*

Now blood was collecting at his boot. Inara somehow had drawn even closer. She suddenly grasped the front of his uniform in her fingers. Her chin nudged up, inviting.

"I have never-" Inara began. She was flustered, and her breathing had only grown harsher. Her bottom lip quivered but her eyes never left his. "Kings...the blood of kings. I can taste them. I have never..."

"Kings?" Ed asked stupidly. "What's that?"

"*Dimmi*," she said calmly, as if she did not realize that she had just grabbed a fistful of his clothes. "Your family…*forse*…is Irish? Scottish?"

"My mother is Dutch," Ed said. "My dad is Irish. But how do you—"

"*Gaelico*," Inara said, smiling. "Yes, Gaelic. I taste in your blood. Your mother, she no tell truth. Or *her* mother no tell truth. No Dutch." Her eyes glittered as her hands dropped from his chest. "*Stai sanguinando!* It is everywhere!"

Ed looked down and saw the red pool gathered at his boot. He stepped back and looked at her pleadingly.

"Do you have a bandage?" he asked meekly. Then, remembering his original mission in a rush of cognizance, he said in a deeper, more forceful voice, "And I need my fellows. We must be off."

She leaned away playfully, as if taken aback. "*O, dio mio!* Hand and foot, no?"

If it was meant as a joke, Ed did not understand. He stood as firmly as he could, clutching the saturated towel around his injured hand. Inara turned with a grin and walked toward the carpeted hallway, motioning with her finger for him to follow. "*Mi sento come una ragazza appena vinta ai numeri,*" Inara said.

Was she speaking to him? Ed leaned in closer to hear her voice. His Italian was poor, even on his best day.

"You know, the game?" she asked. "To play numbers? Is game from South. Coins of wood with numbers. From one to one-hundred. You place coins in barrel, barrel goes round and round. Men bet on numbers. No control. Very foolish."

"A lottery," Ed said.

"Yes!" Inara nodded. "But I say this: *adesso*, with you here… *sento come*…I feel like…I have very rare, most precious number."

"You are too kind, ma'am."

"Inara," she said. "Call me Strega Inara."

The door to which Inara led him was of masterfully cut stone and had a spinning steel bar lock, bolted to both the door and the wall. It reminded Ed of a door to a bank vault. She spun the wheel, and a series of angry clicks and gear grinding ensued from within the mechanism. The granite was a foot and a half thick and must have weighed more than a ton. Yet Inara did little more than brush the rough stone surface with her finger-tips and it opened inward, scraping heavily against stone floor. Inara stood in the doorway and gestured for Ed to go in first. He hesitated, and she let out a peal of girlish laughter.

"Oh no, American Edward. No have fear. Here is place to wait. Here are rooms." She motioned with her slender arm down the length of the darkened hallway. "*Tutti i visitatori mas-chi*...ehh...all men visitors, they go here. Yes?" She smiled. "Even men who kill dogs."

Ed felt compelled to smile back. With acquiescence, he nod-ded, not wanting her to think him foolish. He went in carefully, unsure as his eyes adjusted to the near blackness. For a moment, Ed did not think she would follow.

"*Avanti*," Inara said, her coaxing voice close behind him. Her warm breath brushed against his right ear. She was light on her feet, that was for sure.

As Ed walked forward into the corridor, the long column of yellow light that shone on the floor in front of him narrowed quickly. With the thud of the door closing shut, the hallway was cast into darkness.

The air became much colder once the door was closed. He waited patiently for Inara to spark a candle or flip a switch as his eyes strained to see. Blood dripped with a patter onto his boot.

"Strega Inara?" Ed said. "I really need a towel. And some light, if you would."

Stillness. Ed turned to face her and stared dumbly at the closed door. There was no one behind him.

CHAPTER 3

Strego Bianco

WHEN THE AMERICANS PULLED UP in their truck, Dondio had been watching from the trees. Three soldiers jumped out, while one lingered in the truck. Dondio watched him clean several guns and review the contents of his pockets, waiting for his companions' return. They would never return, of course, and when finally the man grew impatient and leapt from the truck, Dondio had to fight the urge to run over and warn him of the danger. Such foolishness would mean his own death. With a troubled heart, he watched the American square his shoulders and walk into the Strega Nera's lair.

Not long after, Dondio watched the Strega's guards drive off in the American military truck. Once again, they left the headlamps off. The guards would drive it into the river a few kilometers away, as they had with all the others. Over the last week, Dondio had watched many soldiers of all allegiances walk into that gossamer web, thinking it to be a whorehouse. With each passing day, the number of guards stationed outside had increased.

Dondio was as old as his gray beard was long, which he trimmed sparingly using a bear-bone dagger. He wore a knitted cap and a vest of hide laced in the front with twine. His pants were the rough texture of burlap, cut just under the knee for easy riding. A travel bag was slung over his shoulder and his staff was strapped to his back. Dondio never wore shoes, and so was barefoot as he hid in the branches of a pine tree, watching that evil farmhouse for the fifth day. At times he felt that the house's illuminated windows watched him back.

During the day, Dondio watched the guards perform manual labor without speaking or communicating with one another. At night, they stood at attention without rest. Not once did they crane their necks, their heads remaining fixed forward always. A universal vision guided them, their own personal sense of sight unnecessary. This pointed to a very old and evil form of spell-weaving that Dondio hardly could believe still existed. On the day he had arrived, Dondio saw one of the guards fall off a ladder from the second story of the house. The guard quickly tried to stand again, only to have his leg crumple beneath him. Not once did the man bellow in pain or cry for help. He simply continued to rise to his feet and fall again, rise and fall, until he made enough forward progress into the house. Dondio shuddered at the thought of such vile spells, once considered subdued by the *Streghi Bianchi*. This had to be why the Lady of Life had guided him back to his homeland. Inside those farmhouse walls lurked a dangerously powerful Strega Nera.

Twice in the last week, he had seen one man come and go as he pleased, one man seemingly unaffected by the witch's trap. Dondio recognized the man immediately, though years separated their last meeting; it was Giaccomo, now an elderly goods dealer, with whom Dondio had a long history. Dondio resolved to speak to that failed Strego soon.

Dondio had not worn shoes since his childhood in the south, where he had lived before giving himself to The Old Faith, *La Religione Vecchia*. Long ago, a powerful *Strego Bianco* named Filipe had bestowed a quest upon the young and carefree Dondio, charging him to walk barefoot the many miles that separated the port towns of Tauriana and Locri. *Let your feet taste the Earth across the peninsula,* Filipe told his recruit. *Only then will you make acquaintance with the Lady of Life. Then return to me, if you still wish it, and begin your tutelage.* Many things changed for Dondio on that journey. He returned to Strego Filipe as a man. He had grown closer to Aradia than ever before, with feet that were as tough as the thickest leather. His true training then had commenced under Strego Filipe. Over time he and The Lady of Life moved from an exchange of mere acquaintances to that of empress and devoted agent. He had come to know himself through Her. He had cried with Her, rejoiced with Her. He gave himself to Her and in Her grace She nourished him. His dedication to her service was evidenced by his presence in the tree overlooking the farmhouse.

Strego Filipe had warned young Dondio once to avoid confrontation with the *Streghe Nere*. "Wait until you have sufficient support. Perhaps another Strego Bianco or two. You'll need Bianchi strong in the faith. Like young Giaccomo, for example."

Dondio remembered his outrage. "Giaccomo? He's a novice! He'll only hold me back!"

"You both are novices, Dondio. And Giaccomo needs you. You are gifted, with much potential, but remember the Law of Manifold. A Strego Bianco's power is twice as strong when paired with another."

"And thrice with a third," Dondio recited. "But Strego Filipe, I have mastered the fighting arts. I am your greatest student in healing and potions. If I am not ready to face the world's dangers on my own now, when will I ever be?"

"The answer to that is simple," said Strego Filipe. "You won't." His master must have noticed the dejected look on Dondio's face. He put an arm around the young man's shoulders. "What I mean is that you won't know the exact moment. You have grown and flourished through Aradia's guidance. She has shown you light, life, and happiness, yes? Has She not guided you along the path of your fullest potential?"

"Yes."

"And," Strego Filipe continued. "Through Aradia, you have grown to seek knowledge and understanding. Through Her lens, you seek wisdom and truth." The master paused, inspecting his pupil closely. "The Streghe Nere are not like us, Dondio. They are not like you. Malocchio feeds the lower desires of human existence, and those desires feed him. Those caught in the Streghe Nere web come to him with suffering. Malocchio promises to relieve this suffering, but all he does is replace one hunger with another. That is the dark pretext under which the Streghe Nere operate."

"What do you mean?"

Strego Filipe leaned in closer. "Malocchio collects beautiful women," he whispered. "And this brings the men. Honey to draw the ants. And they are all used."

"Used for what?"

"Things vile and perverse. Things for which the Lady of Life never intended a body to be used."

Dondio gasped. He was shocked that his master would speak so bluntly.

"It comes to this, Dondio: Malocchio and his followers seek that which has caused the most corruption of the Streghe, the most corruption of blessed Aradia…avoidance of death."

"I think I understand, master."

Strego Filipe nodded. "Know this, Dondio. Malocchio has power which Aradia has not. The very act of looking into his eyes is dangerous. Men and women lose themselves when they make this error."

A thought occurred to young Dondio then. "Master," he asked. "With a price so high...why would anyone what to become a Streghe Nere?"

"Because Malocchio attracts those who suffer. He finds the ones who hunger, the ones who thirst, the ones who shiver in the wind. While he uses them, they often find wealth and power, and even pleasure in forms. They are fed. But in truth, it is only Malocchio who is nourished. And when he is finished with them, he discards them. Not one of them has lived forever."

Dondio's curiosity must have betrayed him, because Strego Filipe narrowed his eyes. "Do not get involved with the Streghe Nere, Dondio. Malocchio's servants take great pleasure in twisting young Streghi Bianchi."

"I hear your warning, master," Dondio said. "I shall never allow myself to be used in such a way." Even in memory, Dondio ached with renewed pangs of guilt. "And I will guide others away from Malocchio, be it young Giaccomo or any of the other novices, just as the Lady of Life will guide me."

And look where She's guided me now. Dondio shook himself from his reverie and renewed his dedication to the task ahead. He would not watch one more person walk into that trap. As the silent guards drove the truck away into darkness, he slowly climbed down from his hiding place. He needed to understand the full extent of the sorcery. A Strego Bianco such as himself would suffer unthinkable horrors were he caught in the binds of a Strega Nera.

Fog gathered with the falling dusk, and Dondio descended into it as he reached the last branch of the pine and nimbly swung himself onto the soft, needle-strewn ground. He looked up at the fog's white fingers reaching for the eerie, yellow eyes of the farmhouse. With a deep breath, he imagined what he would say to the Strega Nera if he had the chance. Then he laughed. *Foolish old Strego*, he thought. *She is in too deep for words.*

Reaching into the satchel at his hip, Dondio pulled out a small white stone. He rubbed it with his thumb while singing an ancient hymn under his breath.

> *Possa il tuo scopo essere chiaro.*
> *Possa la tua strada essere ben illuminata.*
> *Possa il tuo cuore brillare di luce tra le ombre.*
> *Fluisca il sangue delle cuore,*
> *Fluisca il sangue delle cuore,*
> *Fluisca il sangue del nemico.*
> *Illumina il percorso per un altro mondo.*

The refrain carried the power of *La Religione Vecchia*. As his soft song ended, a dusty yellow Corsican finch fluttered from somewhere unseen. Like a well-trained festival pet, the bird landed into his hand, little stick-legs perched neatly upon the white stone. Dondio whispered to the finch in the Old Tongue, and the bright little bird took wing toward the Strega Nera's house. Dondio directed the bird, not to the sinister windows that looked so much like the angry gaze of a giant, but around to the back of the house, where a smaller paned window was located. None of the guards took notice as the finch landed in the glow of lantern light on the window's edge. Dondio looked into the stone in his hand and saw what the bird saw. It had powerfully sharp eyes for such a tiny creature.

There, sitting in a room cluttered with books, papers, and containing a mirror stolen from the Streghi Bianchi, was the Strega Nera. It was Dondio's first glimpse of her. A beautiful woman she was, with youth to match her intense powers. He studied the Strega hard through the finch's eyes as the woman sat cross-legged in an ornate leather chair. She was in a trance, eyes closed and motionless. She bore the look of both Pia and Elisa.

Memories pounded his mind. Old, sad memories that made Dondio wish The Lady of Life had not guided him here. Any world, any time but here, back to the homeland where he swore he'd never return. Why could not the other Streghi Bianchi be summoned here? Why must it have been him? Alas, the choice was not his. He merely obeyed.

Aradia, the Lady of Life, ruled all Streghi Bianchi, as Dondio willingly accepted when he was Made. As agents of light, warriors against darkness, wizards of goodwill, and servants to Aradia, the Streghi Bianchi acted on behalf of the Lady of Life. Wherever She sent them, they were meant to prevail over corruption and evil. He looked up to the sky and saw the stars fiercely bright in the new night. His resolve immediately strengthened.

I am a servant, I will obey. And I have been hiding from here for too long.

Having seen all he could bare, Dondio called the finch back to him. It came at once, small wings pumping as it made its way back to the tree under which Dondio stood.

No sooner had he reached into one of his many pouches for a morsel of food as a reward for the bird's service, a large form swooped from the tree's cover and intercepted the finch.

Dondio stifled a startled cry as a great owl clamped its talons into the little bird's body midair. He watched, stunned, as the owl glided silently and perched onto a branch above him. It faced him and spread its wings defiantly. Half of the little bird's dusty yellow body bounced at Dondio's feet. The owl puffed its chest, flapped, and gave a guttural cry that made his skin prickle.

Dondio's staff was in hand with the speed of a thought. The owl quickly took wing again, silent as death in the foggy dusk. Dondio spun around, searching the sky above. Nothing. The fog dampened the sound between the trees.

Suddenly, a sharp, feathery mass plowed against the side of his head.

Dondio cried out. He ducked low and swung his staff high. He missed the body, but the thick knot at his staff's end clipped the owl's wing as it swooped. The creature let out a wounded screech and retreated high into the trees.

Blood trickled freely down Dondio's neck. Grimacing, he felt his torn ear. Pinching the skin between thumb and forefinger, he searched for the owl above him. The fog was oppressively thick. The pines whispered, but he could not tell if it was wind.

When Dondio turned, he found himself face to face with the owl. Its eyes glowed in the foggy darkness. Dondio stared into the glowing, golden orbs. Transfixed, Dondio struggled to look away. The orbs grew larger, brighter. The shape of the owl dissolved into darkness, and all that remained were two glowing orbs, slowly merging into one floating sphere of golden light. Distantly, Dondio heard a voice. It was a voice he recognized. Fear gripped his heart, but he could not look away.

"Look, sweet old man. Look, and find what you seek, what you've always searched for. Look and find your lost love..."

Dondio leaned closer. He wanted to find Elisa. He wanted to see her again. And there she was, the dark silhouette of her familiar figure bending to pluck something from the ground. She stood, her silhouette outlined in the glowing golden sphere that grew larger in his vision.

A thought appeared in the blank space of his mind, a prayer for Aradia. He grasped onto it like a man finding purchase on a cliff side.

> May your purpose be clear.
> May your way be illuminated.
> May your heart shine with light in the shadows.
> Flow the blood of the heart,
> Flow the blood of the heart,

Flow the blood of the enemy,
Illuminate the path to another world.

With all his strength, Dondio swung his staff wildly at the shape in front of him. But his staff passed through nothing more than a wisp of fog. His momentum spun him around. Dondio found himself blindly stumbling, vision obscured as if he'd just been staring into a campfire.

The owl was gone, but its purpose had been achieved. Malocchio knew Dondio was there.

CHAPTER 4

The Nineteenth Body

INARA CROSSED AND UNCROSSED HER legs, wondering what her mother would do. She gazed around the room, her eyes finding the small wooden box that sat on one of two matching oak shelves to either side of the mirror. The mirror was a beautiful three-paneled piece of glasswork, and she often found herself staring at it when she thought of her mother.

For as long as Inara could remember, her mother had that mirror. It was full-length and stand-alone, with three panels that folded outward and a silver frame wrought to look like intertwined vines of hedera ivy.

As a girl, Inara had spied though the keyhole into this very room. Her mother had been looking longingly into the mirror, smiling a smile Inara had rarely ever received. Inara had been banned from the study, having been caught more than once trying to get in, and it was the mirror she found most curious. Once Strega Pia was gone, the study was all hers and Inara devoted entire days to admiring her three reflections. They were reflections most unlike those of any other mirror. In each pane of glass, the reflection that looked back was no exact match. They were Inara's images, of course (for who else could it be?), but each inexplicably wore different clothing in styles so foreign she hardly imagined them to exist. Sometimes the reflection in the left pane wore a painted face.

Inara closed her eyes wearily. She could not believe her good fortune. The American's blood left a pleasant aftertaste on her tongue. She had not meant to lick her fingers, but she had felt compelled to confirm what her senses told her. She had whispered one word that shattered the wineglass while the American held it. A simple spell, one of the first she had ever learned, and Inara knew before the first drops of blood hit the floor. It was blood that smelled of the country, of night fire and trees, of rue branches.

Never had she tasted the fresh blood of the Old Folk, though she had read ancient Streghe wizard's tomes discussing its rumored properties. Her mother once had possessed a drop of such blood in an enchanted vial called a *shaelya* that had been handed down for centuries, an heirloom from her mother and her mother's mother before that, originating from a Strega of the Arthurian times named Morgause.

Inara knew the tale of Morgause well. Morgause was the woman who seduced her own brother, the famous Gaelic ruler, King Arthur. In turn, a great hardship was set upon the earth by the incestuous son they created, a son named Mordred, who murdered Morgause before crumbling the kingdom his father had built. The story of the fall of King Arthur had been retold countless times ever since, and it had shaped Stregheria custom. Streghe Nere began to discard their male children after Mordred, for fear of another monstrous mix of Etrusco and Gaelico.

Not all Streghi agreed with this practice of rendition, as it thinned and strained the traditional family lines. Such were the roots of the great split between Malocchio and Aradia.

One side, those destined to align with Malocchio, argued that while the great unexplainable power of the union between Etruscan and Gaelic was corruptible, it was not intrinsically corrupt. Such a union could prove to their advantage, producing beings capable of great power in the ancient magic. Those who would take arms with Aradia cited Mordred as the reason for their opposition, yet they worked in secret to find true-blood Gaelics, who were rare even in those early times. Much more could be done with such blood than merely producing offspring. Dependent upon which sect of Stregheria found these true-blood Gaelics, they were either captured and mated, or simply harvested for their blood.

The Gaelic blood would prevail against those of a weaker lineage, making American Edward's stay less than ideal. Blood of the Old or not, the American was a soldier and soldiers were killers. Why should he be comfortable? Soldiers had killed children in the nearby village. Their parents, with whom Inara had traded tonics for milk and eggs, were all dead. And her dogs... her favorite dog Raldo...dead, all dead. These soldiers, no matter what sigil they wore on their sleeves, all served death. Why should they not serve her instead? They were the real dogs; American Edward would see that for himself. She would let him live. Death and subservience awaited all others, those driven by their foolish lusts. They came at the direction of an old man, Giaccomo, a long-since failed Strego who would do anything for the sensation of escape and the promise of restored youth. Giaccomo was a disgusting wretch, a man destined to join her population of *corsi* as soon as his usefulness was spent. Malocchio's vile magic had its purpose, and employing it, Inara put all men to good use.

The killing of men could be such a mess. So, she let men do the killing for her, since they were so good at it. They came to her driven by lust, and she penned the beasts to let them have at each other. Whether out on the battlefield or locked in her dungeon, they'd be killing each other anyway. This way, she could safely retrieve the body, evoke the spells Malocchio had intended for his *Streghe Nere*, and build the strength of her own protection. Two of her protectors stood rigid and silent in the shadows near the door to her study. At any given moment, they were ready to serve her commands.

"Slave," she said in her native tongue to the one on the right. "Fetch my moon box."

The statue of a man suddenly came to life. Like the protectors outside, his helmet was low to the bridge of his nose in a manner that would have obscured the vision of a normal man. He made his way across the parlor directly for the oak shelf that flanked the mirror. However, with his first step, he began to hobble and sway from side to side.

"Stop!" she commanded, and he immediately obeyed. "What is the matter with you? Answer."

"My ankle is broken, mistress," the guard said flatly. "I was obeying your orders to repair the window ledge. You did not order me to fall, but I did. I have failed."

"You have," she said sharply. "Were you expecting to retrieve my moon box, walking like that? What if you had dropped it?"

Unprompted to respond, he remained silent.

"Die," she said flatly, her eyelids fluttering with annoyance. "But do not soil the carpet."

The soldier's knees gave out and he crumpled to the floor, once again nothing but a corpse. The helmet tipped off and bounced up against the wood panels of the wall. The soldier's empty, black eye sockets blankly faced the ceiling.

"Slave," she said to the other motionless figure. "Remove him and return with another. And make sure the next one is useful."

Wordlessly, the second soldier bent over the motionless figure and effortlessly lifted the body. He carried the dead weight on his shoulder with a straight back, one arm wrapped around the lifeless soldier's torso, showing no more strain than one taking a leisurely morning stroll. He even stopped to bend down and pick up the helmet. Inara basked in the knowledge that she had control of such slaves while her predecessors had not. She could be more powerful than the great Streghi of Old, who had wasted so much time with concerns of *Bianchi* versus *Nere*.

"And close the door," she added, smirking.

The slave reached back and quietly shut the door behind him. Inara sighed and got up to retrieve the wooden box herself. She wet her lips as she drew her thumb along the ancient wood grain.

Chin low to her chest, she brought the box back to her chair. Passing in front of her mother's mirror, the hedera ivy pulsated and shimmered, catching the light on their silver leaves. Inara ignored the distraction and sat with the box on her lap. The tracings of an eye were carved into the lid, framed by six curved lines: three above and three below, intended to show the reach of Malocchio's vision. Not only could Malocchio see into the human mind, the doings on earth and into the heavens, but he could also see purgatory, the realm of ghosts, and those cast into the darkness of Hades. *A lot of good it did him*, she thought, *trapped inside Inara's Moonstone.*

Inara reached over to the small end-table next to her cushioned chair to a jar of cut crystal. She removed the lid and reached her hand inside. She had enchanted this dish to keep perishables fresh with a spell similar to the *shaelya* vials used by her predecessors. Setting the lid aside, she peered into the bowl, searching for one that was not smashed or misshapen. Satisfied with the best choice, she removed it from the jar.

Pinched between her thumb and forefinger, Inara held a blue eyeball, wet and trailing a thin line of mucus. Her spells were cast with talent, which kept her ever-increasing stock intact.

With eyes closed, Inara hummed softly as she crushed the eyeball over the jagged moonstone. There was a soft pop as chilled goo oozed through her fingers. She patiently coaxed the final drops from the empty, deflated eyeball. The gel formed a long teardrop as it trickled onto the stone. Inara, ever careful, guided the liquid like a baker encouraging the last bit of yolk from an eggshell.

The stone brightened underneath the translucent ooze. Inara carefully lifted it up and peered at it. A mass of swirling clouds appeared inside, and then parted to reveal the moonstone's prisoner.

"Hello, *Master*," Inara said pleasantly. Barring anything else in her daily routine, fanning the demon's temper had become one of her favorite pastimes.

The demon inside squealed with rage, futilely throwing himself against the walls of his astral cell as he always did.

"*Strega Inara*," Malocchio said, with a voice that once had commanded the attention of multiple dimensions, now reduced to the high pitch of a small child. He spoke in the ancient Tribal Rasenna, his language of choice. "*I've sent my larè and you have ignored it.*"

"The owl?" she said with a laugh, continuing in her native Italian dialect. "I'm not one to speak with birds. That would be uncivilized. Besides, how am I to communicate with an owl?"

Malocchio let out a high-pitched howl of rage, displaying his clear limitation of vocal variety. As she was pleased to watch, Malocchio attempted another escape. It was a dance they'd done before, one that she expected. Beams of light burst from the stone, aimed directly into Inara's eyes. It was a maneuver of the dark Master's that would ensnare most creatures to his will, Streghe and laity alike, but Inara expertly averted her gaze, rendering it as harmless as candlelight. The effort drained the demon's energy, and Malocchio collapsed back in Inara's spell-woven cell, heaving in exhaustion.

Moonstones were used as communication between Streghe. Ten years before, on the day she killed her mother, Inara also succeeded in capturing Malocchio inside that same moonstone through which he had given Mother her orders. Inara, a girl of sixteen, had trapped one and killed the other, all in one decisive motion.

It had happened in the woods not far from the farmhouse, in a grove where her mother had built a modest altar. Pia had been kneeling in the moss, speaking to a voice that carried through her moonstone. Inara had been just a girl, but the adults had underestimated her potential. In their greed and desire to have her for their own ends, they had disregarded her intellect, her dexterity, and her growing power.

Her attack on them was not perfect. It was a dagger for Strega Pia's neck, and then a quick pivot to use her magic on the moonstone. She was gifted, but they had many centuries of experience to her mere sixteen years. The dark Master's reflexive response nearly tore the flesh from Inara's bones. Her own power managed to block his curse just barely, but the outburst of energy shattered the moonstone.

Strega Pia's body, already dead and burnt in Malocchio's rage, was torn further apart by moonstone shard shrapnel. Inara spent the next day picking the bits of moonstone from her mother's corpse, and months thereafter searching the land around the altar for any lone shards she may have missed. The largest piece Inara kept for herself, and she used that now to view her captive demon.

Once trapped, Malocchio could perform no harmful outburst as he had done in their first encounter. Still, Inara could not suppress his strength of will. Eye contact through a moonstone, even though the smallest shard, would be enough to force even the most powerful Streghi to fall under his will. Even animals could be taken, which explained the owl that circled the house as of late. The curious bird of prey must have somehow found one of the moonstone shards near the alter.

In the ten years since his capture, the owl was the fourth bird Malocchio had managed to control of which Inara knew. *Those winged creatures are damned*, she thought, *by their attraction to anything that carries a glimmer in the moonlight.*

"You are a fool to refuse me," Malocchio hissed in his little voice. "*Many things happen that your eye overlooks.*"

"What could it be?" Inara asked. "News of rodents, *Signore* Owl Master? Are there some especially fat ones in some secret spot only the owls know, grown large on dead soldiers? Honestly, I care little for the affairs of avian creatures."

"*You have a Strego Bianco outside your walls. An old wanderer who knows his power well. Those such as he always appear where Gaelic blood mingles with Streghe Nere.*"

That the trapped demon could already detect the lineage of American Edward concerned her, but the information about the Strego Bianco was equally worrisome. Loath as she was to admit it, Malocchio was correct about one thing; the Streghi Bianchi were written to appear when Streghe Nere met Gaelico. This had been true ever since their founder, the famous and mighty Strego Maerlyno il Bianco, failed to prevent the first disaster between Morgause and Arthur.

"You are a liar," Inara told him flatly. "A desperate lonely liar, oh Master of Owls and Rodents."

"*Have you decided what you are, fool of a girl? Serve you Black or serve you White?*"

Inara laughed. "I serve the red."

"*Your clever jokes do not help you now. Only my knowledge can do that. Release me, and together we can defeat the Strego Bianco!*"

"I defeated you and Mother easy enough."

"*You sprung a coward's attack from the shadows. Release me and I will help protect the Gaelic soldier. The Strego Bianco will kill you both!*"

He's baiting me, Inara thought. *Even trapped and near powerless, he always is working some trick. He wants me to attack the Strego Bianco in his stead, if there really is one out there, and get myself killed to make way for his escape. Despite all, he still thinks me inadequate. Well, that is what I have my Nameless Ones for. I will command them to watch for this Strego Bianco, and Malocchio shall remain imprisoned. The demon is not the only one with tricks.*

Inara was suddenly tired of playing with the once-powerful demon.

"Inara," Malocchio purred like a tiny kitten. "*I can help you build an army of protectors, far greater and more powerful than you could imagine. No harm shall come to you. Ever. Think of what you've lost, and what you stand to gain.*"

She normally did not allow him to converse with her this much. "And how many nights will pass before I am smothered in my sleep, the way you've smothered the ones that came before me? I've read the tomes, Master Owl. You forget, I am not your prisoner. It is the other way around."

She abruptly closed the box, sealing Malocchio's prison and silencing his high-pitched protests. Death or freedom – those were always the two choices available. American Edward, with his true Gaelic blood, was her freedom. American Edward brought her a chance to break the gossamer web of Malocchio's curse that was woven into her own lineage by her Streghe Nere ancestors.

Turning their backs on Aradia, the Streghe Nere had made a pact with the demon. In exchange for their pledge of undying servitude, Malocchio granted them the power to shed an old body for a new one, and thus the potential for eternal life. With American Edward having so fortuitously come to her doorstep, Inara now had the means to sever her bloodline's tie to the demon altogether. She would need help to perfect the delicate steps of this dance.

Already she had shattered convention; she was to have been Strega Pia's nineteenth body.

CHAPTER 5

1 Tuoi Pantaloni

"HELLO? MA'AM? STREGA INARA?"

Silence. Perhaps there was some mistake and the woman had simply gone off to fetch his men and would soon return. Ed lingered in the hallway, and minutes passed with no change. Slowly, his eyes adjusted in the dark, and Ed began to make out the end of the long hall. Nursing his cut hand, Ed pounded on the stone door with his other. The block of granite was so thick, his strikes hardly made an audible sound. With a sigh, he turned and began to walk the length of the hall toward the dim, gray illumination at its far end.

Groping for possible explanations in his mind, Ed hoped the woman was not an enemy. She was an Italian, her accent made that plain, but it was only a few years earlier that the Fascists had ruled here. She could be a Fascist sympathizer, or some sort of madwoman...or maybe just a whore displaced from Rome like the old man Giaccomo had claimed. This could be no more than a foolish misunderstanding. Perhaps he was too fresh from battle to discern social cues, like being caught out of practice at deciphering word puzzles in the college paper.

His troubled thoughts were cut off by a scream that echoed off the dark stone surrounding him. He instinctively pressed his back against the wall, listening as the screams continued. Soon Ed recognized that the cries were not of pain but of scolding. It was a man yelling at someone, or maybe two people fighting.

He began to walk toward the light with his good hand feeling along against the wall. As he inched closer, the faint light grew in strength. Ahead, the hallway ended and made a sharp cut to the right. The screams grew louder and were accompanied by the shuffle of feet. *Trouble with the whores,* he wondered. But no, this was no whore's voice. Carefully, Ed peeked around the corner and saw another, shorter hallway that opened to a room at the end. It was from that bleak room that the light and the screams emanated.

Ed crept closer, consciously placing each step so that he made as little noise as possible. He began to make out the words hidden within the screams.

"You block-head! Get your own damn knickers, you fucking Guinea!"

In response there was a deep grumbling, words in Italian maybe, but it was spoken too fast for Ed's ear to catch.

"Ow! You cock-nosed, swine-runt bastard!"

In the room, lit dimly by a single bulb hanging overhead, Ed saw a naked man sitting against the wall, chained at the wrists. The chains were bolted to the stone at a low point, at about the height of a grown man's waist. The naked man sat on the floor with his arms hanging straight out at the shoulder and his legs outstretched, his little member hiding in a mighty tuft of sandy hair and pinched shamefully in between his thighs. At his feet was another man, neither chained nor naked, who was crouched over and working intently at … something.

The chained man was facing Ed. He was skinny, with blond hair and hearty stubble about his face and neck. Ed could see that the chained man wasn't *completely* naked; his pants were in a bunch around his ankles. He continued to cross his feet in an attempt to stop the crouched man from taking them off. Ed's eyes met with the chained man, and he could see the man's instant relief.

"Yes, you there!" the mostly naked man called, clearly the Englishman that Ed had heard from the hallway. "A help, per-chance? This dago seems bent on my britches. Believe that?"

The crouching man turned suddenly to Ed and hissed. He was small and round and had the look of a pauper. The pants the man wore were indeed rather shabby.

"He's a bloody nut!" the Brit said. "Be careful, friend!"

"How did you get down here?" Ed asked as the pauper rose to his full height, which was barely five feet.

"The fucking witch!" the Englishman yelled back. "Same one that put you down here! Am I right?"

Ed didn't want to answer. The pauper edged closer.

"*I tuoi pantaloni,*" the pauper growled.

"Pants?" Ed remembered that word, at least.

"*Maledica la strega. Dammi i pantaloni.*"

The little Italian approached carefully within arm's reach. His eyes were blood red and leaky. A fine black hair seemed to coat the man's entire body, clearing out only for the purpose of eyes, nose, mouth and ears. A small, stocky chest heaved as if winded, but the clenched fists suggested he was ready to do whatever was necessary. When the Italian stepped closer still, Ed drew his sidearm. He winced as the fresh cut on his finger contorted with his grip. The wound reopened like a squeezed envelope. More blood trickled down his arm.

"Back up," Ed said. To his surprise, both the pauper and the Brit began to laugh.

"Won't work in here, friend," the Englishman said. "Figured you would have known already. Thanks for the thought, though.

Plenty more of the useless things over there." He gestured to the right with his head. There were a number of firearms in the shadow of the room's corner. The light was so dim that Ed hadn't noticed them before. "They're bewitched."

The Italian made his move then, while Ed's head was turned. Impulsively, Ed aimed the gun at the little man's chest and fired. The gun clicked once as the trigger froze against the inside of the barrel.

The crazed man launched forward and swung into Ed, knocking both men to the dirty stone floor. The Englishman was screaming something, but the sound became muffled. The Italian's torso covered Ed's face like some sinister pillow. Ed pushed hard with his arms. But the little Italian was surprisingly dense. Ed's right hand was bursting with new pain. He felt the wet slick of blood as he tried in vain to heave the Italian off.

Unable to gain any leverage with his legs, Ed felt panic inflate his chest. Ed's nose was pushed viciously to the side. He thrashed and kicked. How long it had been since he'd had a breath? When he began to feel dizziness, a sudden last effort flamed through him.

Perhaps the small man was tiring, because when Ed heaved forward, his adversary gave somewhat. Ed took advantage of this small space to turn his face forward and clamp his jaws onto a mouth-full of soft flesh. The Italian howled like a maniac and tried to pull off. Ed's jaws remained clamped. Ed felt hot blood trickle down his throat. One more frantic scramble, and finally the man rolled away.

Ed and his opponent were lying on the ground next to each other, both gasping for breath. Ed's mouth was full of bitter salt. He spit. As soon as his breath slowed, he used his arms to inch away from the crazed Italian. He became aware that the Englishman was still trying to talk to him.

"Shut up," Ed told him.

The Englishman did shut up, and Ed turned to the Italian, who was rolling on the ground with his arms crossed protectively over his belly. Tears stormed down the little man's dark cheeks. The square room had no furnishings of any kind save for a few barrels that stood in one shadowed corner. The little pauper began to crawl his way toward the barrels.

"He'll work up his nerve and come at you again," the Englishman said. "I been playing this game with him for God knows how long now."

Ed ignored him, his gaze never leaving the whimpering Italian. He was beginning to realize what this was. He had been captured by the enemy. Sargent Reynolds was wise and Ed hoped he'd get the chance to tell him. This war was not over.

"Hello?" the Englishman inquired. "Dear friend? A moment of your time?"

"I said shut up," Ed snapped. "I've just been captured, damn it."

"Oh, sorry," the Englishman said. "Do excuse me. My, am I rude! Would it help if my dick stood up and performed a musical dance number for your pleasure? Just to relax your nerves since you've just been captured and all. Bet you'd like that. Me personally, I'm tired of looking at my dick because my pants have been bunched down at my ankles all afternoon." His voice rose and gained a maniacal fury with each new word.

"Down at my ankles! With a fucking mad cell companion waiting until my eyelids droop and then *cominci!* Not a bloody wink of sleep in days. But hell. My apologies for the bother. You fucking wanker."

Ed grunted and got to his feet. "All right, all right," he said. He approached the Englishman carefully, as if he were some beast on display whose manner of killing was as yet unknown. Ed grabbed the waist of the trousers and at arm's length pulled them up the Englishman's hairy legs.

He turned his head away from the Englishman's bare middle section, monitoring the Italian still sulking on the other side of the room. When he was finished, Ed stood up and faced the chained man.

"Button those, won't you?" the Englishman asked politely.

"Fuck you," Ed said. "That's plenty well enough to keep the theater closed tonight."

The Englishman choked a laugh. "I like you already. You're a prick. Funny, I always hated American pricks like you back home. Seems I've had a change of heart."

Ed smirked and felt the dried blood crack on his chin. He began to scratch at it with his fingertips.

"You look like a demon," the Englishman said. "Face full of blood. That how Americans are winning the war? You blokes trained to bite now? Savage."

"He jumped on me. I couldn't breathe."

"Hell, I'd have bit him too. I was just joshing you, so no need to go sour. I think you saved me, you know. I'm grateful. This is a story we can tell our grandkids one day, after the war. Let's leave my dick out of it though. Hey!"

Ed turned his back on the Englishman and began to pace the room. The Italian was sprawled aside the barrels, occasionally uttering a muffled sob. The gentle swaying of the singular hanging light bulb cast shadows in constant movement. Ed tried to think as a military man, not as a helpless captive. Somehow he had lost that train of thought within the confines of this strange house.

"Hey! Where is your sense of decorum? I was talking!"

"Then talk to me about something important," Ed said. "You know how to get out of here?"

"Does it look like it?" the Englishman rebutted.

Ed pinched the bridge of his nose between two fingers. "What about Inara?" he asked. "How did she capture you?"

"Well, I thought I was going to bone her. Same as you," the Englishman said with a sad smile. "I mean, could you *imagine*? I'd still bone her."

"I didn't come here for that," Ed said. "I came for my men. Three of them. There more cells around here?"

"Bet there are," the Englishman said. "But I don't know. I'm chained to the bloody wall. See?" He jingled his chains as proof.

"Why are you chained?" Ed asked with sudden suspicion. He gestured with his thumb over his shoulder. "And why ain't he?"

The Englishman glared at him from the very tops of his eyes. "Ask the witch," he said. "She's the one that's been playing with us the whole time. It's torture, is what. War crimes."

"So you were in chains the whole time?" Ed persisted. "Since the beginning?"

The Englishman sighed. "No, I strolled in just like you. There was another man here first. His name was Marlan. He'd been alone for a while. Things between us went… sour." He looked away from Ed and fixated on something on the floor. "Marlan went mad, like our fellow over there. He attacked me, I fought back. And then she came and… took him."

Ed grimaced. "Took him?"

"He was dead," the Englishman said. "She waved her hands. That was all I could see. She waved her hands and then he got up and left with her."

"Then she threw you in chains?"

"No, then another fellow happened in here. He was all right at first, and then he soured as well. And we quarreled a bit and—" The Englishman paused and looked to Ed. "I know it sounds bad, but you still have your wits about you. I did what I had to, I—"

"And then she came and took that one too, the second one you killed?"

The Englishman nodded sadly. "That's when I went in chains. Seems I've overstayed my welcome." He snorted a pathetic laugh.

Ed glanced back to the injured Italian. "Then he came along?"

"My executioner, more or less," the Englishman said. "Not quite the hooded man with an ax, is he?"

"So why am I here?" Ed said, to himself if anyone.

The Englishman did a hanging-arm shrug. "Clean-up crew? Take us both out and clear the way for more? The corpses become her guards, you know. I'm sure of it, now. By God, it's nice to actually say it out loud, rather than just in my head."

Ed leaned hard against the stone wall and slid roughly to the ground. He positioned himself so he could see the Italian and the Englishman at the same time.

"Now that I'm no longer nude," the Englishman said. "I feel a proper introduction is due. I am Howard Norton, Captain... I have an estate outside of London."

"Edward Layne, Private First Class. Iowa."

"I should have been a Major or a Lieutenant-Colonel. But you Americans don't have any taste for British class, and I imagine you don't want to hear my pitiful story of how I was robbed of my career advancement in the expat colony of coffee plantations in Kenya. So. Let's talk about something we have in common. How many of those hairy-lipped German bitches are going to be raising orphans because of you, Private?"

Ed kept his head down. "Surprised you talk like that," he said. "I hear the Krauts treat you Brits quite nicely."

"Nicely?" the Englishman said, as if insulted. "Haven't you heard of the firebombing of London? Where have you been? Or can you not read? In all seriousness though, how many notches on your belt?"

Ed gave him his cruelest glare. "Three," he said.

"Me, I shot eight. And blew a good dozen to bits with grenades." The Englishman laughed again. "Can't tell you how many of those dogs I've shot too."

Ed's eyes bulged in shock. "You shot those dogs in the road?"

Howard's mouth took on a sarcastic frown. "I didn't shoot them *all*," he said. "Those things are like monsters. Rabid wolves, or worse...Much more of them up north."

"I'm coming from the south," Ed said.

"Right, well, so was I. We hooked back around and then came across this cozy little stop. Thought I was doing her a favor, with the dogs. Those mongrels should have three heads, for how vicious they are." He laughed to himself. "Needless to say, the witch wasn't grateful."

"She was kind to me," Ed said flatly. "Nice, even."

"It matters not," Howard said slowly. "She wants more soldiers, you see."

"Like the ones outside? Those fellows were strange."

"You could say that," Howard said.

Ed frowned. "Are they really corpses?"

"Mind if I close my eyes?" Howard asked, ignoring Ed. His eyes were already closed. "If you'd keep watch. Bastard dago hasn't let me sleep in, well… "

The Englishman appeared to have drifted off. Ed couldn't tell if it was sincere or not, sudden as it was. For a while, Ed sat and watched both men. His mind flashed from subject to subject, image to image, like a broken movie projector going haywire. Wright, Arnold, Oaks. Elizabeth, Sargent Reynolds, the Germans he'd killed, those dead dogs in the road. Tears began to well, and he made to put his hands over his face when he noticed the still-oozing slash on his finger.

He cursed his own stupidity for not tending it sooner, and went right into tearing a strip of cloth from the cotton shirt he wore under his fatigues. Ed sat on the floor and tried to estimate how much blood he'd lost in the last hour. That was no doubt why he was feeling waves of dizziness and nausea.

Ed had his hand in his lap, carefully wrapping the injured finger, when he heard the quick rustle of moving feet. He turned to look, and his temple was met with a stinging bare-fisted blow that whipped his head around.

The Italian was weak, or else such a blind-sided blow would have knocked Ed out cold. Ed rolled and stood up as the snarling little man charged at him again. Ed was ready for him this time and caught the little man in his arms, flinging him to the ground. The man cried out, but quickly recovered and charged again. Ed pushed him off.

"He won't stop," Howard said groggily.

Ed tossed the Italian down each time he charged. Soon Ed realized he was backing into a corner, the corner that was stacked with firearms. Ed darted back and grabbed the first rifle he could reach. He held it up butt-first, like a club. The little man paused for a moment. With a grunt, the Italian charged.

Without hesitation, Ed swung the rifle handle into the man's face. There was a sickening crunch, and the Italian fell hard onto his back, instantly motionless. Ed's breathing was quick and harsh. He leaned a hand against the crumbling wall to brace himself. His wounded hand burst with pain. Ed pulled away and cursed, stomping his foot. Luckily, the Italian was done moving.

"Get over here," Howard said hoarsely. The Englishman seemed to have lost strength in the last few minutes.

Ed held his injured hand close to his stomach and walked close enough to stand just outside the range of the man's legs. Ed's head was throbbing.

Howard looked up to him with tired red eyes. "Keep your distance now," he whispered. He gestured with his head to the still man. "She knows when a prisoner dies. She'll be in for him soon."

Ed could barely hear him. He plopped down against the wall next to Howard. They each sat, both watching the Italian's body, a dark pool forming around the small man's head. Howard's eyelids hung low, and Ed realized that this man was so sleep deprived that, at even the slightest prospect of safety, his body had succumbed to sleep. Ed wondered what it would be like, not to deal with just one maniac in here, but three, as Howard had done. He silently sat next to the sleeping Englishman, hoping he would not have to find out.

CHAPTER 6

Good Boy

SARGENT LEOPOLD REYNOLDS HAD TRACED his four missing men to a little hole-in-the-wall pub on the outskirts of Ferrara. The bar girl directed him to an old yokel sitting at one of the crooked tables. His name was Giaccomo, who told him, in broken English, that a group of American soldiers had left the bar yesterday evening, raving about a whorehouse they had discovered.

"Better be some damn fine whores," Reynolds said with a frown, scribbling on his notepad. The old man grinned, toothless, fumbling at a trinket that hung around his wrinkled neck.

The sergeant was thirty-one, and four years ago he had taught history and coached a baseball team in Missouri. He wore a thick mustache that he tugged on compulsively, especially when in deep thought. Like so many other men, he had only one desire—to return home. Reynolds looked at this goal very systematically. Each achievement on the field was but a rung in the ladder off this continent and back to Eastport, Missouri. His home was a little town that he had come close to loathing before he had been forced to leave it.

For what must have been the thousandth time in that hour alone, he cursed his four missing men. It was rare for him to come out personally to search for soldiers that were M.I.A., but the fighting was finished here and life in camp was stagnant. *If you want things done right...* he told himself. He relished the thought of catching those boys passed out drunk on some Italian whore's floor. He would put the fear of God into them.

Reynolds and his three men loaded into the jeep and rode silently to where old Giaccomo had directed them. There were not many people on the military road; a young woman and a child, an old man riding a small white filly. Local activity.

The missing men had not been seen since yesterday around sixteen-hundred. If they had broken down, their jeep would be on the side of the road. If some other fate had met them, he supposed they'd see it by the light of the following day. The evening fog was becoming more dense.

"You don't suppose," Private C.J. Waters said, his hands gripping the truck's steering wheel, "that they were attacked...do you, Sarge?"

Reynolds shook his head slightly as he yanked at his lip hairs with one curled finger. "There's no insurgency here, not anymore. The Brits have men to the north, and they've been through this area up and down."

"What about that British commander? He said they've had men missing from patrol."

"That was a few weeks ago," Reynolds said. "If there was some band of Krauts hiding in a barn taking shots at Allies, they'd have moved on by now, or gotten themselves killed."

"I know, it's just-" Waters broke off and sighed. It was not customary for a Private to speak so candidly with a superior of Reynolds' reputation, but Waters had earned Reynolds' respect in Sicily. The sergeant thought the young man was sharp and held a great deal of potential. "It's the radio that bugs me. Anything could've happened, really, but the fact that they didn't even get a transmission over is mighty worrisome."

"They wrecked," called up Private Jim Boston, who was seated behind Reynolds. "That's what we would'a thought on the Ohio State Patrol. I used to have to drive up and down highway 80, to Columbus, watching the ditches, sharp turns, the thicket, ponds. Especially in the winter. Hell, we should be doing that."

Waters gestured to the scenery before them. "Fog's too heavy. And everything's flat around here anyway."

Boston shrugged and stared out of the truck defiantly.

Near the spot they expected the whorehouse to be, Waters brought the jeep to a halt. A fresh dog corpse in the middle of the road had attracted a group of scavengers. Around the dark lump stood four live dogs. They were painfully skinny.

"Corso," Reynolds said. He leaned out of the truck for a better look.

"Good looking dogs when they're healthy," said Waters. "Smart too. The Romans trained them for war."

"Yep," Reynolds agreed. "These ones are rabid, though." Indeed, a white froth clung to the four dogs' jaws like dainty little beards. They watched as two corsi took giant bites of rotting flesh, while the other two dogs paced around the decaying corpse. The creatures were so hungry that their eyes appeared to have sunken into their heads and were covered in shadow.

After a while, Reynolds spoke. "Morrell," he called behind him.

"Sir," the private named Morrell said.

"Put them creatures out of their misery. Poor fucking things."

"Sir," Morrell said in compliance. He was a lean, bony kid of twenty years, and when he stood up in the truck he seemed to tower over everything. He raised his rifle, closed one eye, and took aim. The men waited for the shot, but it never came.

"Rifle's jammed, sir," Morrell said.

"Jammed?"

Private Boston passed his rifle up to Morrell. Morrell set his own aside and inspected the new rifle briefly before raising it to aim again.

"Trigger's locked," he said, bringing the rifle back down. His brow was creased with confusion. "This one won't shoot neither."

"Bullshit," Reynolds said with annoyance, grabbing for his own gun docked next to him between the door and the seat. "Don't you girls check your weapons? Did you both just get off the bus?" He too gave his rifle a quick eye-over before rising in his seat. He leaned over the windshield and propped his elbows there.

Reynolds cursed. Inspecting his rifle again, he lowered himself back into the cab. There was nothing wrong with the weapon. Two of the dogs stared at the newcomers questioningly with deep, dark eyes, jaws chewing mouthfuls of flesh.

"Sabotage?" Reynolds asked himself, fingers raking his face for hairs to grab on to. "I'll be bitched. Check everything, men."

The men were checking each firearm they carried, aiming all the while at the dogs. The trigger of each weapon held steadfast against the inner barrel as if it had suddenly welded in place. When the jeep's engine died, each of them sat dumbstruck for a moment. Waters tried the engine once, twice, and nothing happened. Next he tried the radio, with the same result.

Boston spoke up. "Lookit," he said. "We got more of them mutts coming from behind us."

Indeed there were. The men saw three packs of dogs, each coming from its own angle toward the jeep, dozens of dark glares fixed upon the soldiers.

"The fuckers are surrounding us," Reynolds said, stroking his mustache even more rapidly with his knuckle.

The dogs that closed in wore the same white beards of foam. Sharp ribs could be seen from under their tight fur. Fur that was tattered and patchy, as if each animal had survived a battle. The corsi formed a perimeter around the jeep, with one especially tattered-looking dog inching forward on Reynolds' side. Not one of them barked or growled, and each kept its tail tucked between its legs, as if its protection was of the utmost importance.

"Go on, get!" Reynolds called. He took off his helmet and waved it at the nearest, snarling dog. It recoiled and regarded the waving helmet curiously. When it determined no threat, the corso crept closer.

"Good boy!" Waters suddenly called out. Once more he tried to get the engine to turn over. It would not. He punched the steering wheel, causing several the dogs to jump back.

"That's it," Morrell said. "Throw something at them. Something loud to scare them. I'm not getting out to fix this truck with those bastards out there."

The men looked through the jeep for something of little value. In one cargo compartment, Boston found a warped metal pot. He stood up and tossed it hard at the ground, hoping to make it bounce. It hit at the rocky edge of the road and bounced as he had hoped, but the dogs were not frightened. Instead, they leaped into attack, mobbing the flimsy, little pot with such malice that the soldiers bunched closer together. And they attacked in silence; no barks, no growls, no snorts, just the dry bone to bone snap of their jaws and the jostling of their starved bodies.

As a group continued to fight over the inedible pot, more dogs appeared at the edge of the fog. The corsi collectively moved closer. It was now or never. With a rush of adrenaline, Reynolds stood up and assumed command.

"Men! Your knives!"

Each man drew their issued eight-inch blade, which most men kept on their boot. Reynolds carried a machete of sorts, twelve inches of steel with teeth, which he kept on his belt whenever he was afield. He held it out before him as he rummaged through his pack with his free hand. Reynolds pulled out an extra pair of army trousers. He held out his left forearm and wrapped it with the trousers, forming a padded guard.

"What about the bayonets?" asked Waters turning in his seat to get a better look at the weapons.

"You need two hands. One to attack, one to guard. Get your forearm as bulked as you can," Reynolds said, and the others followed his example. "Hurry. Hold out your left arm like a shield, and direct that pad right at their jaws. If they clamp down on you, cut their fucking guts out. " Everyone moved quickly. When there weren't enough extra clothes. Morrell and Waters were forced to take off their shirts.

The dogs were now gnawing the tires. The acrid odor of rubber wafted in the air, along with the repulsive smell of decay and the musky smell of wild animal.

"God be damned for a grenade," Reynolds breathed. But as he said it, he knew those might not function, either. The guns, the truck, the radio; something had disabled all their equipment. It all seemed as purposeful as the teeth waiting behind the pack's curled lips.

"I got me attacked by a dog once," Boston said. "On my granpap's farm. Protect your face and your cock."

Even Reynolds flinched when a dog clanged onto the jeep's hood. Its nose wrinkled in a vicious, silent growl as it bent its hind legs, prepared to pounce. A tremor went through the whole of Reynold's body. What he had taken for dark, sunken eyes was something entirely different.

The dogs had no eyes.

CHAPTER 7

Elisa's Eyes

Dondio passed another truckload of Americans on his ride to Ferrara. They were heading for the Strega Nera's trap, he was certain. His heart yearned to stop them, to say something, but his task was urgent. They would never listen to someone who looked like an old hermit anyway. He would be best served to find Giaccomo. If it was as Dondio suspected, the spineless old bastard was sending troops to the Strega in exchange for some reward.

The white filly did all the work. During the ride Dondio saw the fog begin to form in low crevices. The sky went a burned orange before it darkened, and moisture fell to coat verdant blades of grass with drops of dew. Old memories stirred with the setting sun, as they so often did since his return to Italy. They were memories of Elisa, lost so long ago.

He thought about her often, in the most basic lover's way; what her voice had sounded like as she spoke sweetly, how her hands gestured with her words, the lavender scent of her curly auburn hair.

Dondio had been traveling. Through unfavorable circumstances, he'd found himself in Ferrara.

Frustrated, separated from a sizable bag of gold, and wanting solitude from his inept traveling companion, Dondio had started off on a brisk walk to clear his head. His feet carried him along a road, which in turn became a path, which in turn became a trail through the countryside. There was a grove of trees beneath a sloping hillside, and Dondio made for its cool patch of shade. As he stepped into the mottled shadow of the overhanging branches, the most beautiful song reached his ears.

Her back was to him and she was knelt before a pond, singing in a beautiful low tone. He remembered thinking then that The Lady of Life had given him a gift for his loyal service. During his travels Dondio had been able to take in more than a few operas in France and Italy, and he would have sworn then, without any sort of emotional prejudice, that the girl by the pond had the finest voice his ears had ever heard. He was in love with her before he even saw her face. It was an old song of *La Religione Vecchia*, a song penned before the Schism between Bianco and Nera, an innocent song of sweet love and birds and trees. *If you were a lark and I was an oak, would you fly to my branch and sing? Would your song accompany the wind in my leaves, if my leaves keep the rain from your head?*

When Elisa saw young Dondio approach, she abruptly cut off her song and made to flee, holding up her skirts in the rush. He was much quicker than she, and he sprinted around the pond to block her escape. The girl looked startled and she held her out hands defensively. She wore a plain brown dress and a green shawl. The hood framed her beautiful face loosely, allowing locks of curly hair to fall against her pale skin. Her eyes, green like polished gemstones, were wide with alarm as she spoke.

"Go away!" she said. "I am a Strega and my gift is your curse!"

"Please," Dondio replied. "I'd accept anything from you, gift or curse."

The two exchanged a long look. Dondio, young and unchanged by his trials, looked much different then. His hair was cropped short and his beard was but stubble. He'd been a handsome lad, much to the chagrin of some of his fellow Streghi Bianchi. Elisa seemed to think this too, as her face warmed visibly as they looked at each other. Suddenly Elisa's gaze broke, and she pushed past him and darted through the trees and out of sight. His heart nearly burst from his ribcage to follow her, but something in her look told him it would not be wise.

Dondio returned to the pond the next day on the exact same hour and found her there again. She was kneeling at the water, and she looked up at him with timid eyes, as if she both expected and feared that he would come. Without slowing pace, he walked directly to her and sat down. By the end of that day they were lovers, and by the end of that week they were inseparable. They often slept by the pond together and watched the sun rise through the trees. Elisa absorbed knowledge of Aradia from him and in return she taught Dondio many wonderful things. It went on like this, on and on, for a few wonderful months. A season of Elisa, he often mused.

One day, Dondio met Elisa at the pond as usual, but she was crying in great miserable sobs. He set down the flowers he had picked for her and rushed to catch her in his embrace. When she quieted, he asked what was wrong and the sobs resumed in earnest.

She gathered herself enough to tell him that she was pregnant. Dondio's initial feeling was of insurmountable joy. To hell with the Lady of Life and with Malocchio. Let them fight their own battles. Here was the sweet soul he so desired, Elisa and no one else, and he was lucky enough that she carried his child.

It was not so, she told him. Her mother would never approve. Elisa explained things to him that he already knew but had chosen to ignore in love's blinding light. She was a Strega Nera, and Streghe Nere did not have consensual relationships. Their mate was selected for them by their mothers, based on a wide variety of factors that were fathomable only to the witch herself. When Strega Pia discovered what she had done, and with *whom*...

Dondio blurted out a thousand protests, a thousand options the couple could take. He told her how large the world was, how many places the two could go and raise their family outside the relatively small orbit of *La Religione Vecchia*. He could see that none of it was getting through to her, but still he persisted. When that did not work, then he begged.

She told him no, she would not go. She resolved to tell her mother it all, for better or ill, and that she would return to him at their special pond as soon as she could. He kissed her sweet lips one last time and she turned and walked home through the forest, his eyes watching her until she was gone from sight.

More than a week passed before Elisa returned. Dondio had been camped out at the pond, anxious, with stomach cramps and uncontrollable sweats. He spent the majority of his time waiting, constantly scanning the trees for movement in the direction Elisa would come.

When he finally saw her, he jumped to his feet and rushed over, already thanking the Lady of Life once again. He stopped short of embracing Elisa when he got closer. Something was terribly wrong.

"Elisa?" he said breathlessly.

Her face had never been as blank as it was then. Her emotion, which was normally as easy to read as the weekly papers, was gone from her face. His chest crushed painfully when he noticed her eyes. They were no longer that crystal green, like stained glass. They were a deep, dark brown. They were not Elisa's eyes.

"Witch!" he accused, his anger flaring in an instant. He reached back over his shoulder and snatched his staff, the same staff he carried now into old age. Elisa's face remained cool, but her hands rose as if pushing an invisible foe. Dondio saw there were new additions on her hands as well, an oval-shaped tattoo on each palm. The hair on the back of his neck stood on end. He recognized the mark. It was the sign of the evil eye of Malocchio.

The words Elisa spoke then, and the alien tone of her woman's voice, had replayed in Dondio's head every day since.

"I am Strega Pia," Elisa's mouth said. "The mother of the girl you raped. Elisa is mine, was always mine. The child you gave her is mine. Strego Bianco filth!" She spat at his feet.

Dondio tried to hold his staff before him as he was trained and conjure all the protective magic he could quickly muster. Rage was too great for patience; he charged at her with a cry. Pia clapped her hands at him, a horizontal motion that mimicked the clamping of some carnivorous beast's jaws. Dondio felt an impact and was taken off his feet. His back hit the rough forest floor and he lost all breath. As he gasped for air, a great weight pressed down on his chest. He tried vainly to move, but the Strega Pia possessed powers for which he was unprepared.

"While unconventional," she said. "You have actually suited my needs quite well, Strego Bianco Dondio della Religione Vecchia. A Strego papa for Elisa's little child! Much more promising than the cattle-hand she would have been mated with. Next best thing from a Gaelic is your blood."

"Elisa..." Dondio managed.

"She is gone. She was bred to be my shell and that is all she is or was. Normally I take their bodies before I mate them, so I can have the fun of it. Another thing you've denied me." The Strega was on her hands and knees now, nuzzling her face in the nape of Dondio's neck. She smelled him and licked him, murmuring and snickering all the while.

"Thanks to that vile root between your legs, I've been forced to occupy her much sooner than I'd hoped. Fourteen years is the soonest I've ever had to do it, you debaucher."

"Fourteen?" Dondio blurted. He had no idea Elisa had been so young. The Strega Pia released her magical grip just so she could indulge in his reaction.

The Strega Nera's smile was as frighteningly beautiful, sincere, and pleasured as a smile could be. "Yes," Pia said. "My daughter's cunny was only fourteen. Are you a fool, Strego?"

Dondio said nothing.

She giggled at him. "Elisa was a charming little one, beautiful like a woman already. I knew she'd be a problem with the menfolk. She was plainly advanced, but-"

Pia pointed at him and laughed like a schoolchild, drawing her finger from his brow all the way down until she circled it around his naval. "I underestimated her, and so did you, fool! Or perhaps you *overestimated* her." Pia laughed harder.

The magic lifted from him, and Dondio sat regaining his breath.

"Dondio," Pia said, now firm in tone. She lifted her skirt and brought a leg over his body, straddling him. "I will kill you if you follow me. Stay away from my home and my child." Pia moaned softly as she licked his face, lapping like a kitten. "I do wish I could have been there. I'm so much more proficient than Elisa was."

Dondio lashed out at Pia with all the magic he had. For a moment, when Pia's brown eyes widened in surprise, he thought maybe he'd succeeded. Those thoughts were quickly dashed when Elisa's sweet smile returned.

"You are no fun," Pia said, standing up. "The Streghi Bianchi are a dull folk. Just remember, return my favor of not killing you. Walk away on those ugly bare feet. Do not follow me. Go your way and forget all this." She turned and made to walk off.

"Wait!" Dondio said. He got back up and went after her. She did not even turn around before he was again thrown to the ground. The pressure of her magic quickly returned, horribly intensified. Dondio felt one rib crack, then another, and he gurgled a scream through blood that filled his throat.

"I had hoped this would only be a talk," Pia said, returning to stand over him. "But you do not seem to understand. Killing you now would be wisest, but perhaps you can serve as messenger to other pious Bianco priests. Your kind should keep their distance from the Nere. Keep your eyes down and your swords sheathed, or both will be cut out. If you're not convinced perhaps you need some time to think about it."

A stab into his right side, a sickening twist of his innards. His reflex was to curl into a ball and scream through the pain, but her magic prevented both. He sprawled on the forest floor, writhing like a worm on sunbaked bricks.

"That horrible pain you are feeling," Pia said. "Is the equivalent of an eight-inch serrated blade dancing in your bowels. You have until sunrise to enjoy it. Do think about those things I told you, Strego Dondio. Maybe ask your Lady of Life for counsel on how best to scream. Ciao." Her laughs faded into the distance, echoing through waves of pain that pulsed through his bones.

It was a night of agony, sharp fire and burning knives.

At sunrise, the magic suddenly faded. Dondio lay gasping for breath, sweat dripping from his face. How long before he could move, Dondio could not tell. First one arm, then the other. Stiffly, he tried to sit up, but all his strength gave out and he crumpled to the ground in sobs. It took until the afternoon for him to gather himself and set out to somewhere far away.

That was twenty-five years ago on this Earth, though it felt like a great many more years than that for Dondio. *I knew I'd be made to face it,* he thought as he rode the white filly toward Ferrara. *Before the Lady was to be done with me, I've always known She would send me be back.*

As he entered the war-torn, walled city of Ferrara, Dondio wondered if Giaccomo would even recognize him. He rode directly to *La Terra Grandisima*.

Dondio did not bother to hitch the filly outside, nor did he carry rope or harness. He simply leaped off the animal and walked into the tavern.

Inside the tavern was dark, the dusty shadows punctuated with dimly glowing orbs of candle light. Two large men sat at a table in one corner. The bar stood against the opposite wall. A petite serving girl looked up at him from her intense cleaning. He walked toward her.

"This place is too expensive for you, old man," one of the men called over to him harshly, in southern Italian dialect.

"No, it's not," Dondio said. "I've got plenty enough to tip. Your name, m'dear?"

"Crista," she said. "But I don't get any-"

"Get the tip jar, if he wants to tip," the man at the table said without looking up. Then he muttered something under his breath to his companion, who laughed obnoxiously.

Dondio nodded to the two men, and then turned back to Crista, surreptitiously sliding her a five lira piece.

"For you," he said softly.

She pocketed the coin as Dondio dropped two coins into an empty jar she set on the counter. The coins fell and rolled inside with the loud notes of metal on glass.

"All we have is whiskey," Crista said apologetically.

"Biggest you have, please," Dondio replied. "And I need some twine and nails. Is that old goods dealer about?"

"He's got a room upstairs," Crista said. She poured his glass full. "Don't bother him, though. He'll come down when he comes down."

Dondio nodded. "This place is so empty. Where are all the soldiers?"

She shrugged. "Some Americans just left. They were talking to Giaccomo before he went to sleep. We usually don't get crowds for another two hours or so."

Dondio took a gulp of whiskey. "Giaccomo? Friends with soldiers?"

Crista gave him a patronizing look. "You know what they wanted. Same thing you do, too. You're just going to have to wait for your whores. It all goes through Giaccomo. And he's sleeping." She did not try to hide the disgust in her voice.

Dondio leaned in, not wanting the two men to hear. "Ten lira if you go get him from that room."

The girl made to say something, but her eyes averted to the floor and she stepped away. Dondio looked over his shoulder and saw the man who had spoken earlier approaching.

"Get away from my girl, you disgusting old man," the muscular brute said. He wore a tight white shirt, military issued pants and boots. His eyes were bloodshot, and a vein pulsed in his neck.

"Friendly conversation, really," Dondio said. When he faced the man he saw the soldier was a good head and a half taller. The man looked down at him.

"Is that an old goat sleeping on your chest, or a beard?" The man spat on the floor. "Where would a hermit like you find coin?"

"My meager savings. Nothing more."

"You don't even have shoes," the man said. "If you had any savings, you would buy some for yourself." The second man then got up and circled around behind Dondio.

"He's a thief, Alberto," the second man said. "We should confiscate his loot."

"Or turn him in to the Americans," Alberto said with a smile. "If he's been thieving there might be a reward."

"No need for any of that, gentleman," Dondio said. "Just an old man here, looking for some company."

Alberto looked him over and rubbed his own hairy chin. "Tie him up," he said to the other man. "Let's have the soldiers get a look at him."

Many things happened at once. The man behind Dondio made a swift movement to grab his left arm. Dondio jabbed with his right fist at Alberto in front of him. The impact broke the large man's nose and forced him back a few steps. Before the man behind him could react, Dondio spun out of arm's reach. Dondio lethally swirled his staff in both hands. In one fell swoop, the staff smacked one man and then the other with bone-cracking precision. Their bodies hit the creaky wood floor with consecutive thumps.

Each man had a bloody dent in his skull. Their legs jolted and kicked as Dondio rummaged through their pockets. In one of Alberto's pockets he found a small sack stuffed with coins and tied tightly. He tossed it onto the bar, and the coin-purse slid toward Crista's trembling form, mostly hidden behind the large counter-top. Her tiny, watery eyes peeked up at him over the bar.

"Your employer is deceased," Dondio announced. "I'm sorry. I'm sure you needed this job. Hope this money helps."

The girl suddenly stood straight and wiped her teary eyes. "No one will care," she said. "Nobody's really left to care. Everyone always hated him." She clenched her fists in quiet rage. "I hated him."

Dondio gave a slight bow. "Pleased to be of service, dear. Now, Giaccomo-"

"Upstairs, third door on the right," Crista said quickly. She gave a strange little smile. "I hate that old pervert, too."

Dondio spun his staff in his hand and gracefully sheathed it on his back. "That makes two of us. Anyone else staying up there?"

"No," she said. "Haven't had real boarders in months."

Dondio smiled. "Thank you. Be safe."

"You too."

The two went in opposite directions, Crista for the door out-side and Dondio for the steps to the rooms. He bounded up the stairs into a dark hallway, narrow as the staircase, with three doors on each wall. Dondio's eyes worked wonderfully in the dark. The door Crista specified was the only one closed. Dondio loved it when childhood skills became relevant in things that mattered, and he went to work picking the simple lock. As a child, before *La Religione Vecchia* and training with Strego Fil-ipe, he had had no choice but to steal food, clothes, and other needs. As a self-trained expert, Dondio had yet to meet a lock that could resist him.

He pushed the door open slowly. Through the blackness, Dondio could make out the figure lying on a bed at the far side of the room. The stench of whiskey and wet tobacco was thick. A bottle lay on its side with its contents pooling on the little table next to the bed, then dripping onto the floor. The drunken fool must have bumped it in his slumber.

Dondio paused. He noticed a wide spit-pot on the floor next to the bed's old, splintered headboard. The blankets rose and fell in tandem with gentle snores. A mass of gray hair covered the pillow.

Dondio took one giant step into the room, snagged a fist-full of hair, and pulled. Giaccomo woke with a scream of surprise. Using strength that did not match his lean, sinewy arms, Don-dio pulled Giaccomo onto the floor and held his head over the absurdly unattended spit-pot.

"Greetings, tradesman," Dondio said nicely. "Glad to see you well and sleeping so soundly."

"Alberto!" Giaccomo managed to cry. "Uri! Help!"

"Those men are dancing with the devil now, Giaccomo. Hope you have your Sunday shoes with you."

"No!" Giaccomo said. "Who are you?"

"Fluisca il sangue delle cuore, fluisca il sangue del nemico," Dondio recited the refrain of the Strego Bianco song.

Giaccomo gasped.

Dondio forced Giaccomo's face into the inch-deep bowl of tobacco phlegm. The old man tried to fight, but only succeeded in covering both sides of his head with the brown goo.

"What did you say?" Dondio asked. "I can't understand you when you're chewing. Speak clearly."

Giaccomo spit and breathed heavy between words. "Curse you, Dondio. What do you want? There some old crime I have yet to pay for?"

Dondio leaned in close. "I don't care about the goddamn gold from twenty five years ago. It's your recent crimes I'm here about, shepherd of Malocchio. I want to know about the Strega."

"Strega? I know no Strega. You're the Strego."

"You could have been a Strego, too, you fool. You chose your path. But this time you go too far. You send the men, Giaccomo. To their doom. Does the witch pleasure you in exchange? Or does she just let you watch while she enjoys the company of someone less decrepit?"

Giaccomo snorted a laugh. "You are a bastard, Dondio." His toothless gums smacked with each syllable. "But I know of no witch."

Again, Dondio forced him into his own standing saliva, for much longer than before. He pushed harder too, driving the man's face painfully into the shallow pot's metal bottom. When Giaccomo's struggles became violent, Dondio relented and gave him some air.

"Honesty, Giaccomo. You know what the Strega is capable of. I can do much more than that right now."

"Damn her," Giaccomo slurred in defeat. "What did that elf-eyed bitch tell you?"

"Elf-eyed?" Dondio said with a raised brow. "What do you mean, elf-eyed?"

"You know, green. Like staring into a damned swamp."

Elf eyes. Dondio felt such a profound shock that he almost let go of the old timer.

"Brown," he said. "Pia has brown eyes."

"*Inara*," Giaccomo corrected, wiping his nose. "Has green eyes. Long, dark hair. Angry as sin."

By the tradition of the Streghe, Pia would have raised Dondio's daughter and gone on to inhabit that daughter's body by now. That meant the Strega's eyes, or truly Pia's, should be brown, not bright and flaring like green glass, not the beautiful inherited eyes of Elisa. *Unless Pia never was able to take Inara's body...*

Anger for his lost love and daughter blazed with sudden ferocity. He grabbed Giaccomo by the wrists and spun him onto his back. The old man let out a whimper of fear.

"Her guards," Dondio growled. "Those are the soldiers you sent there, no?"

"I don't know. "

Dondio shook Giaccomo. "Do they have eyes?"

Giaccomo's own wide eyes stared up at Dondio in fear.

"Does she pull out their eyes? This is important. Does she?"

"Please let go," Giaccomo wailed. "Just let me go. I will tell you."

Dondio relinquished his hold, and the old man pushed himself up. "I can tell you all, more than you thought possible-"

"Out with it, then."

"Just...just let me breathe..." Giaccomo gasped for air. He reached for a blanket on the bed and wiped his face.

With a sudden flash of metal, Giaccomo pulled a knife from under the bed covers. He lunged at Dondio, uttering a guttural cry. Dondio dodged and kicked. The knife went skidding across the floor. Giaccomo fell back down, cradling an injured hand.

Dondio reached down and grabbed the old man by the collar of his shirt. "Does she," he growled through clenched teeth, "pull out their eyes?"

"Yes!" Giaccomo coughed as he struggled.

He abruptly dropped the old man. Giaccomo flopped onto the floor like a limp fish.

"How?"

Giaccomo coughed and looked directly up at Dondio as he shakily sat up. "I show you, okay?" He held both hands up. "I show you, just don't hit me." Reaching one hand down the front of his own shirt, Giaccomo pulled out a necklace with a white orb pendant hanging down the center of his chest.

"She sees all," Giaccomo wheezed, holding up the white orb. It spun slowly in place, dangling from his fingers. As it rotated gracefully in midair, a cloudy blue iris spun into view. The hair on the back of Dondio's neck stood on end.

"She gives me money, I talk up her whorehouse." Giaccomo coughed again. "I'm not her pimp. I'm in promotions, like Hollywood."

"When does she look in?"

"At night, usually. Just as the crowd is coming in. So she can see who will be…who I will send." Giaccomo's brow was damp, and he reeked of sweat and fear.

"How do you know it is her?"

"Because…because the eyeball turns green. She told me to take it out when…" Giaccomo shut his own eyes, and a look of disgust crossed his face. "When it starts moving."

Dondio stood over Giaccomo, watching the eyeball-within-glass spin, a mesmerizing, white orb hanging delicately from a small token on the crude necklace chain. He wondered if it were possible that somehow the cycle was broken and Pia was no more. Inara might not be a dark witch, a cruel Strega Nera. Instead, she might be a frightened young woman, his *daughter*, protecting herself from war with the most powerful spell-weaving she knew. Abruptly, he snatched the white pendant from Giaccomo.

Dondio turned to the door, tucking the pendant down his own shirt and taking out his stone to call the white filly.

"Wait!" Giaccomo cried. "Don't go!"

"Oh, yes," Dondio said. "What was I thinking?" Dondio walked back across the room to the bed. He bent down over the blankets and ripped a length of fabric.

"To stop the bleeding?" Giaccomo asked, holding up his hand.

Dondio smiled. "To stop the talking."

Giaccomo cried and fought back, but he was too weak.

Once the old man was tightly bound and gagged, Dondio walked out of the room and did not turn back again.

Dondio and his white filly sped north, off of the road. He had plans to circle around through the woods and come at the Strega Nera's house from a different direction. Everything was drastically changed in his mind, and he only thought of one thing.

Green eyes. Elisa's bright green eyes.

CHAPTER 8

The Strega's Conscription

E D NEVER TRULY FELL ASLEEP, but a bright light stirred him from his exhausted state. He moaned as the pain in his hand returned, and when his eyes refocused he saw Inara standing there. She frowned, a vast difference from the girlishly-polite woman that greeted him when he first arrived.

"Thank you, American Edward," she said plainly. Her green eyes glared at him like a stern mother.

"For what?" he croaked.

"This." She gestured down to her feet, where the Italian was spread out on his back. "Now he can be useful."

"I didn't do anything wrong," he said. "Neither did my men. The war is over. Let us go."

A smile came to her lips. "War no concern. My one concern is ... *blood*."

"Blood ...?" Ed's memory flashed an image of Inara licking his blood from her fingers.

"I am lucky woman to have you. Future was dark. But then you arrive. I promise you no hurt."

"I want my men," Ed said, the strength of anger gathered him to his feet. "I want my truck. American soldiers will come looking for us, and you'll be cooked when we're found. Let us go."

Inara sighed, as a mother would during a delicate lecture to a child that simply did not understand. "Men will come, more men will come. You no leave, American Edward. You are mine." The giggle that followed was one that under other circumstances could snare a man's heart. Here it made Ed cringe. It made him resolve to hear Beth's laugh again.

"Where are my men?" he said.

"American Edward, you have fear."

Inara squatted over the prone body. "This man worse than animal," she said. She spat at him. "Disgusting man." She spread the fingers of one slender hand over the still face. The corpse convulsed. A light formed under her hand, and as it grew brighter it pulsed like a beating heart.

The corpse's limbs contorted to unnatural angles. Each muscle within the lifeless body was drawn as tight as a bowstring. Inara lifted her hand above the little man's face, and his head rose with it, a marionette pulled by invisible strings. Inara paused her hand, and then gave a little tug. The head bounced back to the concrete and the body went limp. The Italian's head rolled to the side, facing his fellow prisoners, mouth gaping and eyeless sockets locked in eternal surprise.

Inara stood, cupping the eyes in her hands. She muttered something in Italian. Ed dared not move.

Casually, she turned her attention back to the corpse. "Slave," she said. "Get up and be useful."

The man lurched from the floor and stood at attention in front of Inara.

"Come, slave," she said.

The dead man bowed and made for the hall, affected not the least by his lack of eyes. Inara did not move right away, though. She pondered Ed.

"Water," Ed managed to say. "Please, water. "

A slight smile came to her lips and her eyes seemed to consider. "Give me another favor, yes? Then water."

Ed heard the clanging of metal somewhere else in the room. He turned to look, and was not surprised to find Inara already had disappeared. He saw that Howard, fast asleep, was lying on the ground. Ed looked again. Howard was *lying* on the ground.

Ed shuffled toward the Brit. Above him hung the metal chains, the bracelets cut and bent by some unknown strength. *The witch freed him.* Howard's bony chest rose and fell in his deep sleep. Ed smiled then, a joy for the man's new freedom. He thought about waking him but decided not to. It would be a nice surprise to wake up unchained after a much-needed rest.

Ed reestablished his seat against the wall, facing Howard. With the third man gone from the room, it was not long before Ed's exhaustion overcame him in the silence, and his chin bowed to his chest with his own troubled sleep.

CHAPTER 9

Cycle Breaker

RETURNING TO HER STUDY WITH two new eyes to add to her collection, Inara reflected upon her situation. What if some soldier happened across a shard of moonstone that she had missed? What if Malocchio went riding off in one of those big army trucks before she even knew?

Before American Edward came, she had been plagued with fear. Her slaves and her canines had the area under a tight perimeter now. Yet she needed more. She and American Edward needed protection.

Perhaps she should not have unchained the Englishman, though she was sure American Edward could best him. That powerful Gaelic blood was a force for dispatching foes. She had hoped a demonstration of her power would bring him to her willingly, but he had recoiled, and she had lashed out. *If my power does not convince him, will my cruelty?*

Men ran in packs, like dogs, a fact which she frequently used to her advantage. American Edward's pack was bonded in some peculiar way that Inara could not understand. Perhaps it was something like the bond within a *Buschetto*.

Inara loved her private quarters, although she did miss the outdoors. It was uncommon for a Strega Nera to be as cooped up as she had been. During this war she had done all in her power to stay out of it, to let the kingdoms of men burn themselves without the help of her kind.

Years ago, Inara's mother had been astounded by the progress the young girl had made in her studies of *La Religione Vecchia*. Before she was a teenager, Inara was fluent in more than a dozen languages, new and old, and had read a number of texts that even her mother had blundered through. Pia had frequently been away, often on long errands at Malocchio's bidding. During this time, Inara found herself alone. As a curious child, she gravitated toward the ancient texts in her mother's library. It was during the long afternoons that Inara learned about the dark pact of the Streghe Nere and Malocchio's promise of eternal life to these women. Streghe Nere were supposed to keep their daughters isolated and ignorant of their true purpose. This, however, was Strega Pia's true failure, for Inara learned from the ancient tomes that the only protection available to her now was to kill her mother.

The day Inara learned that she must protect herself or perish was the day she acted. She had seen butchers in the village slaughter pigs with sharp knives. Her mother had twisted and lurched on the ground, desperately trying to keep the blood from spilling from her neck. Malocchio, trapped inside the Moonstone, had no recourse. Inara had felt on the ground with her bare toes and picked up each broken moonstone shard with her eyes squeezed tight. She did not believe the sweet words Malocchio spoke to her. She did not want to live like Pia, shuffling around to do Malocchio's tasks. She would not become like her mother.

Returning now to her quarters, Inara put the eyes away for storage and reclined deep in thought, surrounded by the various instruments of her craft. Many were ancient and of seemingly trivial commercial value, but that made them no less remarkable. There were small stones that could mimic whatever material they touched. There were a set of tuning forks with which one of knowledge could bind a door, completely sealing the passage unless one were able to replicate the exact note. Inara got up from her chair and went to her favorite artifact, her mother's mirror.

The pale face and green eyes that gazed back were familiar. So was the long mane of hair. But in each panel, Inara's reflection showed surprising deviations. In one, her reflection wore hair dyed an unnatural, fearsome red, and eye make-up that consisted of two vertical lines drawn over each eyelid, from mid forehead to cheek, and another horizontal line across the bridge of her nose. Her dress was drastically different as well, reflecting the cultural norms of that other world. It was a tight, darkly-colored blouse over which she wore a red armored corset and a fierce leather cloak that resembled bat wings. Another vertical line was drawn at the soft dip of her bottom lip, straight down her throat where it disappeared into her collar. Long red gloves rode up past her elbows. Inara would never think of wearing such a ridiculous costume, yet the image intrigued her. The woman there looked powerful, a sorceress of great alien magic. The woman *was* her. The *Specchi della Possibilità* were windows into worlds, worlds that paralleled Inara's world in almost every action. Details were mixed up, but similar things happened in those worlds for different reasons. In that pane, that version of Inara had chosen at that exact same moment to look into her own version of *Specchi della Possibilità* to admire her favorite mirror, the one on the left, the one that showed her another world. At that moment, the alternate Inara might have been thinking about how noble and sophisticated the Italian Inara looked in her black dress and wide-pointed hat. In the center mirror, she wore soft garments, tight pants, and her lips were painted red. In the third, her body was covered in a strange gray metal, with blinking red and green eyes affixed to the surface.

As she turned her head this way and that, smiling and batting her long lashes, so did the three unique reflections.

Inara stepped away from the mirrors and gazed out the window to see if the night had brought any problems. By the light of the moon, she squinted to see another military truck, stopped maybe a mile east of the house. Her canines were already on the situation. She smiled and thought of the fancy spell-work involved in imbuing her beasts with machine-stifling magic. Quite clever and practical, she thought. She wondered what her mother would say if she saw her daughter's intricate webs of responsive spells, designed to recognize and attack all types of mechanical devices. By the look of the truck, and the frantic men inside, her spells were woven true. It pleased her, although she knew that cruel pleasure was an aspect of Malocchio's taint.

Inara took comfort where she could. Feeling tired, she left the window and went to nestle into her big leather chair, where she fell asleep.

CHAPTER 10

Twitches

"CORPORAL WRIGHT?" ARNOLD SAID. THE voice was pathetic and small, already choked with tears. "I th-thought everyone else was d-d-dead."

Wright turned his head and met Arnold's gaze. Both of them looked ragged with torn uniforms and bloody, matted hair. Their arms and legs were tightly fastened to separate wooden tables. The tables stood at an uncomfortable angle facing a window that was all night sky and moon.

As for Arnold, his twitch had worsened. His neck trembled almost without cease and his right eye constantly winked as if he had an infinite number of secrets to share. Between these, Arnold could do nothing to hold back his sobs, and he heard himself evoke the help of everyone from his mother to the Lord Jesus Christ. The wooden table squeaked with each of his spasms.

"Pull it together, man," Wright whispered. "I need you thinking clearly so we can get out of here."

"We ain't getting out, Corporal," Arnold said. He sniffed some snot back into his nose. "I had to kill a man. In my cell. I killed him."

"Guess we've had similar stays," Wright grunted. "I didn't get laid either. Starting to seriously doubt that I'm going to." Wright chuckled at his own jest, but it only made Arnold more nervous.

"He was saying something to me," Arnold said. "I couldn't understand."

"Who?"

"The man I killed, Wright! If only we could've talked-"

"Clear your head!" Wright snapped. "And stop twitching!" He lowered his voice considerably. "We need to get out of these ropes."

"Ssshhh," Arnold said. "She'll hear!"

"Of course she will! We still have to escape. Listen, do you know what happened to Layne?"

Arnold shook his head no.

"He had the truck and the guns," Wright said in a loud whisper. "He might have gone to get help. Sargent Reynolds and the boys will level this place."

They froze at the rustling sound of approaching footsteps in the hall behind them. A doorknob turned, following the squeak of hinges.

"Ciao," the woman said, gliding into view. She stood with marvelous posture, wearing a long, skin-tight black dress and a hat that was tall and pointed with a wide brim. Arnold shook like he was riding a boxcar. Her lips bunched in a half-restrained smile. "My goodness," she said. "You have fear?"

Arnold closed his watery eyes tightly and nodded.

"Well, will prove," the woman said. "That I am no whore. That this house is the last place you find woman to spread herself for you. You are wise to have fear." She pivoted Arnold's table so that he was facing Wright. Wright remained stone-faced.

"Look at this one," the woman said, pointing to Wright. "Is soldier. Big, tough soldier man. Who do you call him? Mister Wright?"

Arnold nodded yes.

"Mister Wright. From America. I do not like him, Mister Arnold. I do not like men who search for whores. Very pathetic. But I especially do not like him. He said rude things about me, things gentlemen would not say." She paused for a moment, her smile returning as she played with a piece of her dark hair. "American Edward is much better than you. He did not arrive with you beasts. American Edward wants nothing of whores."

"Fuck," Wright cursed. "Damnit, Ed."

She laughed. "He came to look for you," the woman said. "His men was all he spoke of. Must be noble man. But he is mine now, too. Oh, American Edward. I like very much." She sighed deeply as she walked in between the two tables. Wright turned to her.

"What are you?" Wright asked sternly, looking her up and down from the point of her hat to the hem of her dress. "You look like a witch."

She leaned in closer. "I show you what I am."

She snapped her hands, and a cool liquid poured onto the top of Arnold's hot, sweaty scalp. From the gasp of surprise, Wright was experiencing the same sensation. The cool liquid oozed in lines down Arnold's neck and back, his shoulders and chest, and into his eyes where it burned. The earthy smell reminded Arnold of childhood adventures in the woods, catching lightning bugs and fireflies with his bare hands.

The witch spoke in a soft, sensual voice, a voice that would drive a man wild in a real whorehouse. Her words sounded Italian but were indistinguishable. Arnold's violent twitches creaked his ropes, but despite that he watched closely what the witch did to Wright next.

The witch hunched over slightly as her voice gained volume. Her dainty fingers gnarled into claws and her eyes became burning green flames. Wright's first wail of pain startled Arnold into stillness. He watched as Wright's neck stiffened, clearly not of his own volition. The witch's palm covered the man's eyes and lines of blood began to decorate Wright's cheeks.

"Uno...e...due," she said to herself. Wright moaned as the witch put something into a bowl nearby. Arnold saw two red, bloody cavities where Wright's eyes had once been.

The witch raised her arms to the sky outside the window, as if presenting Wright as an offering to the moon. She cried foreign words, and Wright convulsed. His back rose and slammed against the wood again and again. The contraption showed no signs of giving, even when his movements became sickeningly, violently, unnatural. Arnold turned away, eyes closed, unable to take it in anymore.

"Do you think I'm a whore, Mister Arnold? Look! *Guardami!*"

Powerful, invisible hands grabbed Arnold's head and twisted it straight, forcing his eyes open. He saw the witch before him, her hair frizzled and floating with electricity under the wide brim of her hat, arms spread. She held a dagger in one hand, and Wright was no longer strapped to the wooden table. The rope hung loosely, cleanly cut.

A dog, one of the corso breed the soldiers had seen lying dead in the streets all over north Italy, sat obediently at her boots. Its eyeless sockets took in Arnold inquisitively as its head tipped to the side.

"It's as simple as that, Mister Arnold," she said. "Is much less of a beast now. No problem. Are you ready?"

Arnold cried out, but his neck was locked in one position. His shoulders were immovable too, which kept his constant twitches painfully stifled, but not prevented. His table was pivoted back so that he too faced the moon. He tried to move, but his eyes remained locked on the sky's great glowing satellite. He could look at nothing else. Still his twitch persevered, and his right eye opened and closed despite the increased pressure.

He felt the witch's cold hand slide across the sweat of his hot forehead and bring his eyes to darkness. The full white image of the moon blazed in the blindness. A sweet voice chanted from all directions, and he soon felt very tired. There was a pressure building in his sinuses, and he felt an odd tug. It was a feeling unlike any other in life, as if a person's skull was made of iron and his eyeballs were trying to resist a magnet. Suddenly, the witch's hand came off and she was staring down at him.

"Stop that," she said with an expressionless face.

Arnold tried really hard. Trying to stop his twitching had become a constant task since Sicily. He used the invisible clamp around his head and neck as leverage and tried to tighten his face muscles. The twitches would not stop. The witch cursed something under her breath and replaced the hand over his eyes. Her chanting began anew, along with the strange magnetic pulling, but again the hand came off and sight returned to him. Arnold was met with a glare.

"I said stop that," she said. "*Stai fermo!* Stay still and it will be easier for you."

"I'm trying," Arnold whispered.

The ropes on his hands and feet suddenly released their hold and Arnold's large body crumpled to the floor. The witch pushed him with her small foot and he rolled onto his back.

"Cooperate!" she yelled. "*Ho bisogno della tua collaborazione!*"

"I'm trying! I'm trying!"

The invisible hands took hold of him again, now with a great uncaring harshness. Again his neck stiffened, but his eye could not stop its convulsions. The witch looked down at him with frustration darkening her face.

"*Perché non posso . . .* Why no able-" she said. "What is this? A reflex? Why no able-"

"Sorry," Arnold muttered. "Sorry."

The witch moved closer to him, and she used her fingers to hold his eyelids open. The eyeball underneath continued its dance.

"*Questo no lo farà,*" she muttered. "This no good."

Suddenly, there was the sound of shattering glass and a rush of air. Something feathery cuffed Arnold violently across the shoulders and neck, and he stumbled forward, falling face down onto the hard floor.

The dog that was once Corporal Wright scampered cowering against the wall, whining as shards of glass rained down, tinkling on the floor. A huge owl swooped directly at the witch, screeching loud enough that Arnold winced in pain. For a brief moment, Arnold thought the owl was his savior, its flight path assuming a menacing line to attack his captor. The witch, though, seemed undaunted. The owl's screech cut off with a fluid ripple of the witch's fingers. The bird slammed into the wall and remained there, dangling by some invisible shackles.

Arnold held himself in a feeble attempt to stop the shaking and watched the witch glide easily across the room. The owl went on screeching, despite being pinned, until the calls began to take on a human quality. Was it speaking in a human language Arnold did not understand? The sound was deep and scratchy, but distant, as if its owner was talking over one of the loudspeakers back at base.

"*SSRRAAAA! SSRRAAA! SSRRAAA! SSRRAAA-AARRRRRE you playing with toys while the world ends all around you? Like a child!*"

"Which world is ending?" Inara said pleasantly. "Yours? You have lived too many lives as it is."

"*And I'll live a hundred more. You can never contain me. Underestimating me.*"

"I don't debate with birds," she said. "I tug fine cords of magic and ring their necks." The owl screeched so loud she paused her rising hand.

"*Wait!*" the owl cried. "*Problems in your subterranean prison cells! Go look if you don't believe me.*"

"Problems?" she said with a raised eyebrow. "Of what sort?"

"*Your Gaelic prince,*" the owl said. "*He's dead. I saw it through my larè.*"

"American Edward?" the witch gasped. She straightened and the air in the room suddenly acquired an electric quality. She dropped her arms, and the owl slid down the wall and gracefully found perch on a lamp. She rushed to the door, her face taut with panic.

Arnold, the owl, and Wright the dog stayed in their respective places for a few moments in silence, until Arnold realized he was holding his breath. He let it out loudly. With the witch gone, the possibility of freedom burst into his mind. Perhaps he could sneak down the steps, find the front door and make a run for it. Reynolds would have a search party out by now. Then he could get help for Ed Layne and Oaks, if they were still alive. This could work out for them all. Recovered POW's were often among the top priority to be returned State-side. In a month, Arnold could be on his way back home.

The owl, now free of the witch's magic, flapped over and perched on the table to which Arnold previously had been tied. It rotated its head on a stationary body, turning toward him and freezing Arnold's thoughts. Huge golden eyes came around to meet his and they seemed to absorb every bit of information in that single glance. Then the eyes became less intrusive and more entrancing. There was molten liquid inside the owl's skull, he could see it swirling on the other side of the enormous eyes.

"*There are things, Samson Arnold,*" the owl said. "*That are worse than death.*" Arnold felt himself pulled toward the bird, and he did not resist, did not stop looking through those eyes into the compelling comfort of the swirling, golden fluid.

A moment later Arnold was on the ground again and the witch was back in the room. The owl had been intensely focused on him and had not noticed the witch's return quickly enough. Arnold saw her hand dart out and the owl screamed.

Just then hot air punched him in the chest, and the feathery body of the owl slammed into his face. Arnold's feet left the floor and he felt the window's remaining glass break as he passed through it, the feathers of the owl pressed over his nostrils. Then he was flailing through the cold night air, falling with the ground rising quickly to meet him. He felt the heavy thud of his body hitting earth, but not much else.

~~

THE OWL ROLLED through the air as well, trailing feathers, but once out in the open it was able to stabilize and catch flight. Malocchio extended his wings and caught a draft that raised him higher. He saw the American broken on the ground below and cursed his missed opportunity at freedom. It was no use to take a dying person's body. At least, Malocchio reasoned, he did not lose the body of this fine owl. Among other creatures he had possessed, the owl was one of the best. He enjoyed stalking and hunting as the owl; he relished roaming the night. Perhaps he'd catch a quick meal before he worked on other plans.

Flapping wings that spanned six feet tip to tip, he sent the owl to soar above the trees, scanning for rodents or snakes. Almost immediately he saw a rabbit dart across a clearing. He chuckled at the ease of it and swooped down.

When Malocchio sensed danger and tried to pull up, it was already too late. An arrow whisked through the air and passed through the thin skin of one wing before sinking deep into back muscle. The wing was pinned uselessly to the owl's body, and a great ball of feathers went spiraling to the forest floor.

CHAPTER 11

Playing Possum

Howard's movements startled Ed from his light sleep. Ed first glanced around the room, remembering where he was, then at his hand, which had stopped bleeding but still throbbed painfully. He saw the Englishman struggling to his own feet. The man inched around as if he were first discovering the wonders of walking.

"Morning," Ed said.

"Oh, hello," Howard said. "Just remembering what it was like to walk about and use my arms."

Ed was about to tell him what a piss-poor job he was doing, when a scurrying along the wall caught his eye. A rat, he realized. The dull light bulb overhead cast shadows all about the room, but he could have sworn he saw a twinkle moving along with the critter before it disappeared into a corner shadow.

"Did you see that?" Howard asked.

Ed watched the shadow intently, and sure enough the rat emerged carrying something in its mouth. A sparkling token, a gem perhaps. *Rats don't do that in Iowa*, he thought.

"Rat," Howard said, answering his own question. "The old binomial nomenclature is coming back to me, glad to say. Rattus rattus. You know what else I remember?" He walked with his shoulder to the wall, using it for stability. "I remember why the witch trapped our foolish selves down here."

"What?" Ed sat up.

Howard had made his way into one of the room's shadowy corners. Ed squinted to try to see what he was doing. He rose to a knee. Howard's narrow face broke through the shadow, and he wore a strange look. He walked briskly toward Ed, use of the wall no longer necessary.

"Sorry," Howard said, as he swung one of the dead rifles. Although it could no longer shoot, it proved solid enough. It struck Ed's jaw and dropped him instantly.

"Mother…fucker…" Ed groaned with bloody lips.

Howard rushed in and delivered two swift kicks to Ed's gut. Ed lurched forward in agony.

"You saw what she did to the dago, mate," Howard said. "Nothing personal. You didn't know the rules."

He swung at Ed again, but this time it was blocked. Ed took a firm grip on the barrel and used it to pull himself up. His anger gave him strength through the pain. But Ed's vision was blurred and he could not catch his breath. Howard shoved him hard against the wall, and then kicked out his feet. Ed thudded back to the stone floor. Ed had just enough mind to roll. He avoided the Englishman's kicks.

Ed kicked at Howard and tried to scoot back to the barrels against the wall, not unlike the angry little Italian man had done a day before. This time it won no mercy. Howard brought the rifle down on Ed once more, and Ed went still.

Howard stood, chest heaving, over Ed's body. He turned and walked toward the hallway, knowing full-well the witch would appear. It took longer than usual but, as suddenly and as mysteriously as always, she was there. The witch stood blankly for a moment as if not believing that Howard was standing there himself.

"You're late this time, my dear," Howard said warmly. "I usually don't get this much time with the corpses."

The witch seemed dumbstruck. Her dress was tattered and dirty, and her exquisitely kept hair was everywhere about her shoulders. She looked as if she had just fallen down the staircase.

"The books no lie," the witch finally said. "Is not possible you hurt him. How did you hurt American Edward?"

"Took this to him," Howard said, holding up the bloody rifle. "I win. Do I get to leave now, perchance? I'd be most-"

"No, you don't leave," Inara hissed. "You never leave!" She strode closer, causing Howard to retreat. Her eyes blazed and her fingers were drawn into tight talons. "How did you hurt him? How—"

There was a solid crack; Inara's eyes rolled white and she collapsed. Ed stood behind her, holding another rifle that they had hidden between the barrels.

"Good work!" Howard exclaimed. "A splendid whack! We did it! Well played!"

Although his legs were swaying underneath him, Ed felt a surge of anger and swung the rifle at Howard, not for his head but for his arms and midsection.

"Ow!" Howard cried. "Ow! Stop it! I'm sorry! Ow!"

"That fucking hurt, you bastard. Did you have to hit me that many times?"

"It had to be convincing," Howard said, rubbing his arm. "Told you it would work. Just didn't think she would pop up so fast."

"I can barely fucking think for how hard you hit me," Ed said. He slid down the wall to a seat. "You are an asshole."

"Look, if we get out of here alive, you can tap-dance on my balls for all I care. It worked. Get your shit together and let's take our leave."

Ed glanced over at the witch's crumpled form. She had come to help him. She had been angry that he was hurt. He felt an odd sense of betrayal and shame for tricking her. When Howard had whispered the plan to him, Ed had been skeptical at best. He did not expect to be able to take the witch off guard. But she had seemed frazzled, like too much had happened all at once. She had been unprepared.

The witch's back leg twitched.

"She's not going to make it," Ed said. He went over to her body, ignoring Howard's direction that he most certainly should not. One pale hand lay exposed from under a mass of her pitch-black hair. Ed took the small wrist in his hand and felt her faint pulse for a few seconds. He lost it, and then tried to reestablish his grip, but nothing was there. He placed the hand back onto the floor and sighed, bewildered by his own sorrow. It was as if he had just destroyed some priceless work of art.

"That's it," he said, looking up at Howard. "She's dead. I—"

At that moment the room exploded into gunfire. Every firearm trigger that had been locked was released from enchantment. Stone chips flew everywhere. Howard and Ed instinctively dropped for cover, Ed over the lifeless form of Inara. The ping of ricocheting bullets danced all around their ears, and Ed cried out at a pain in his calve. Howard cried out in a moan that could only mean he had caught something, too.

Once the world settled, Ed raised his head and looked around. The room was filled with smoke and dust. Howard was rolling on the ground, cursing. The pile of guns in the corner was thrown askew; bits of metal and wood carpeted the floor. Ed got up and winced as he put pressure on his right leg. He pulled up his pant leg and was relieved to see an unattractive gash. A graze, not a bullet hole. Next he looked down at Inara's corpse, which didn't seem to have been hit, not that it mattered. Kicking at the debris on the floor, Ed shuffled to the guns and grabbed a luger that looked intact. The trigger was not locked.

"Bloody hell, man," Howard said, rising as well. "I caught some shrapnel in my arm." He held the arm up and Ed saw the raw flesh, peppered with bits of sharp debris.

"Good," Ed said as he inspected more weapons. "Serves your limey-ass right."

Howard ignored him. "So the witch," he said. "Is she—?"

"She's dead," Ed said again. "And I guess whatever spells she made are dead too." A nice-looking German rifle was propped against the wall. Ed looked it over, took aim at one of the barrels and fired. The blast was loud. A hole appeared in the wood and all three barrels rocked. He found another good rifle and passed it to Howard. He took one for himself and began picking through the pistols.

"Stock up," Ed told him. "I've got to find my men."

CHAPTER 12

Animals of Reason

SARGENT REYNOLDS FOUGHT Off ANOTHER wave of sleepiness. He and Private Morrell were hunkered in the cab of the jeep, as they had been for hours, with their backs against the windshield and their boots on the driver and passenger seats. The smell of gasoline filled the air. Reynolds looked over at a shirtless Morrell, who was holding a rifle before him that was now only useful as a club. Both men still had their knives, but they had found the reach of the rifles more beneficial.

The creatures circled the truck, their jaws dark with blood. Hours ago they had succeeded in pulling Private Waters and Private Boston to the ground. There had been no hope in getting between their fellow soldiers and the snapping jaws.

It had been Morrell's idea to use the windshield as a guard, so that the dogs could only attack from one angle. When the dogs jumped onto the truck, the two men beat them back, albeit from a rather uncomfortable position. Still, the line between discomfort and dead was clearly defined. They had managed to drop two of the dogs each, and gave brutal blows to a number of others. Their strategy had worked, but it only served to bring the conflict to a standstill. The dogs had stopped the constant attacks. Instead they paced and waited for the inevitable moment when the mortal men succumbed to their exhaustion and lowered their defenses.

Reynolds tried to focus his droopy eyes forward, the only direction from which he could be attacked. To each side of the truck was a bloody pile that was once one of his men. The smell of blood and raw flesh lingered in the air. The dogs took their aggression out on the truck. The pop and hiss of the first tire collapsing made both men jump. They simply rocked with the deflating of the other three, each popped tire taking them a step lower toward hell. Then, with a fresh wave of horror, they heard scratching underneath the vehicle. The fresh smell of gasoline soon followed. Morrell and Reynolds exchanged a look.

The eyeless beasts seemed more sinister by their silence. Throughout it all they never once barked or growled. The only discernable sound was that of their jaws snapping, as they circled the truck.

"Still wondering what these things are," whispered Morrell.

"Creatures without eyes, creatures from hell," Reynolds breathed.

"They don't bark…" Morrell looked at his commander.

"Creatures of reason," Reynolds mused.

Another four-legged beast leapt up, but Reynolds swung his rifle and connected with flesh. The eyeless face was knocked back into the darkness.

"It makes no sense," gasped Reynolds, "that our equipment should fail now."

"You ever hear of anyone tell about stuff like this?" Morrell asked in a hushed whisper. "You ever heard stories?"

"About creatures from hell with no eyes? About radios and rifles not functioning?" Reynolds paused. "No," he said. "Never."

"Then we might not make it out alive, sir," Morrell's voice quavered, fear lumping in his throat. "If no one lived to tell... we might not make it out..." Morrell's voice trailed off, and Reynolds stood to swing at another set of snapping jaws.

Both soldiers had faced battle, had seen men run for their lives in futility. But even across the disarray of a war zone, that chaos obeyed certain rules of nature. Mechanisms failed all the time, always at the worst possible time, but there was always a reason.

Morrell had managed to snatch a small piece of a metal bar, probably from a tent pitch, and tried desperately to pry the trigger of his rifle. It would not budge, as if it were bewitched.

Reynolds watched, and then gazed off into the darkness. Here he was, a family man who had fought his way across Europe only to be killed *after* the war had been won because of some other soldier's dick. Wright, Oaks, Layne, and that immature Arnold had been looking for a whorehouse because at least one of them couldn't control his cock. Normally Reynolds wouldn't care in the slightest where it concerned his soldiers' cocks. He just hated to die over the post-pubescent urges of some impulsive little grunt.

Reynolds would have snapped his fingers were both hands not locked in a death grip around his rifle. Arnold's promotion. That's what the men were doing, they were celebrating! A wave of goosebumps went up his back to the hair on his neck, and was followed by a drowning guilt for his negative assumptions. They were soldiers, in war, trying to have a small piece of real life. Reynolds remembered his own real life. Backyard picnics and lemonade, and playing dominoes with his daughter. Working on the shed on hot weekend days. Moths bumping the backdoor window at night, the soft armrests of his chair in the den, the murmur of the radio mixed with his wife's soft snoring as he drifted to sleep beside her.

At the loud crack, Reynold's chin snapped up from his chest. He felt a vibration in the rifle he held, the echo of a shot fired. His nostrils filled with the smell of spent gunpowder. In the dim starlight he could see white smoke rise from the truck. A few firearms tumbled from their resting places on the back seats. Reynolds startled and held out his rifle, ready to swing. Confused, he saw that all was calm except for a buzzing sound. He realized it was the static of the radio come back to life.

"Morrell?" he cried in confusion. "Morrell, what the-"

Morrell was slumped face-forward into the passenger seat, a bullet wound to his neck. Reynolds glanced down at the gun in his hand and paused. He put a hand to Morrell's bare shoulder and turned him slightly. The hand came back with warm, dark liquid.

"Morrell!" he cried again as he flipped over to sit in the driver's seat. "You there, soldier?"

Reynolds turned they key, still in the ignition, and the jeep started up with a kick. There was still a remnant of gas in the tank. He resisted the celebratory holler in his throat but he could not contain a smile as he felt around for the headlights switch. He found it and the scene illuminated before him. His jaw dropped open and for a moment he was unable to move at all. The beams revealed several naked men, curled into themselves like sleeping children, lying about the road and in the field beyond. The men looked to be sleeping, but Reynolds could not imagine how they got there. And where had the dogs gone that had swarmed around the jeep for the last few hours? Those naked fools would be eaten right up.

The shock of what he saw quickly faded as he recalled that he now had means of escape. He must find a way back to camp. Then he would return with help. He shifted and got the truck moving. Carefully he maneuvered around the men, unsure whether they were alive or not. He already had the responsibility of two lives on his hands, his own and Morrell's, and that was enough for one man.

He spun the wheel with one hand and tried to stir Morrell with the other in hopes of getting some sign of life. It pained Reynolds to recognize the obvious, that it had been his rifle, slumped carelessly in fatigue, which had suddenly fired and hit Morrell. Every locked trigger in the truck had fired; he was lucky to have not been hit.

Whatever had crippled their machinery had thankfully lost its influence. Reynolds pressed hard on the gas pedal. In response, the jeep lurched forward on flat tires in the direction of camp. The radio was his next priority, once he got moving. He reached down for it in between the two front seats, but drew his hand back when he saw the torn metal of the box, and a few wires. The radio had been hit in the gunfire and was sputtering. Instead he continued to reassure Morrell, despite his fear that the man was beyond hearing. Just in case, he kept talking.

It was no more than a minute before the engine sputtered. Reynolds held his foot on the gas, but a few seconds later it sputtered again, then stalled, and died completely. The wheels rolled the truck quietly before it lost its momentum, and stopped. Reynolds caught the strong scent of gasoline.

Reynolds listened closely for the sound of the dogs before he jumped out of the truck, his rifle held before him no longer like a club, but in the correct fashion. The night was silent aside from the chirps of insects hidden within the countless blades of grass. There was little wind. He spared only glances as he inspected the truck, and kept his eyes on the road.

The gasoline smell grew in intensity as he circled around the truck's rear. He saw exactly what he had feared. Under the rear passenger-side wheel well, the bottom of the gas tank had been ripped open. It still dripped.

Animals of reason, Reynolds thought. Camp was a night's walk away. He did not like his chances out there with the beasts around.

He kept his rifle ready to fire as he walked around to Morrell. There was no movement from the body. Reynolds tugged at his mustache, hard and purposeful. That hint of pain went to his head, clearing it. He strode to the truck bed and grabbed all the weapons he could carry. Now armed with two rifles, two pistols, and a belt of extra ammunition, he took off on foot toward his only chance, the closest shelter he saw, a house by the edge of a small copse of trees, blanketed in dense fog.

CHAPTER 13

The Healer

DONDIO GRIPPED THE ARROW'S SHAFT and pinned the lump of bloody feathers down with his bare foot. A sharp tug freed the point from between two rib bones. Though the large bird was clearly dead, its eyes remained opened wide, as if it could not accept its fate.

The *larè* lying dead at his feet was not the end of Malocchio. The Strega Nera was still a slave to her ancient Master. He gripped the arrow tightly and looked up at the stars, the eyes of the night. If Pia was indeed gone, he swore to save his daughter from the taint of Malocchio that slowly ensnared all who practiced *La Stregheria Nera*. It was the dark curse of the evil eye that would gradually corrupt from within. Dondio breathed out heavily. He reached up with his free hand and pulled his hood over his head.

With the stealth of an experienced hunter, Dondio weaved his way through the trees and brush.

He circled around the house and approached from the east side where there were no windows. Against that wall of the house stood five guards, equally spaced and at full attention.

He had just begun to plan his attack when he heard a snort. It was no hog or corso. When he heard a soft sob he rose to his haunches. Carefully, Dondio's sharp ears lead him closer to the source, and he began to hear the hiss of whispers. The sounds were coming from a place closer to the house and in direct view of the great windows that overlooked the lawn. Pausing, he noticed that the windows at the house's front were broken. What had he missed during his visit to Giaccomo? As he approached the last few trees before the clearing, Dondio saw a dark form in the grass ahead, about halfway between the house and the edge of the forest.

When the wind picked up a little, Dondio clearly heard what the whispers were: Christian prayers, spoken in American English. They were the very basic prayers, nothing fancy. A jumble of Our Father's and Hail Mary's and incoherent pleas to be saved.

No, he thought. *She wouldn't be that reckless. And no one could survive…*

Despite the possibility of being seen, Dondio hunkered down even lower and slithered into the grass like a serpent. He made directly for the dark human form in the open field ahead. His legs were directed to the body but his eyes never left the guards. The guards, however, made no movement.

Upon reaching the man, Dondio immediately rolled next to him on the rough ground. The man let out a loud shriek and Dondio hushed him.

"Who's there?" the man said in a shaky, but whispered voice.

"A priest," Dondio said. "Tell me what happened? Quiet, now. Where are you hurt?"

In the moonlight, Dondio could see the man trying to turn his head, but his neck would not move. Dondio could also see, with the faint light reflected off the man's cheeks, that he suffered spasms every few seconds.

"Jesus Christ?" the man asked. "Is it you? Is it over yet?"

Dondio reached out and put his hand to the man's chest. He felt sharp pieces of glass in the cloth. This man had been tossed from the window, and a good distance at that.

It was clear from the man's lack of leg movement that there was spinal damage. The wet snorts told Dondio there was internal bleeding, possibly punctured lungs. There was only one chance, and it would cost Dondio precious energy. That sort of spell-casting took time. A guard on patrol could come walking along.

Lying there on the ground, as close to the Lady of Life as possible, it would be blasphemous for him to reserve his skills. Dondio reached into his pouch and after a brief rummaging he pulled out a small diamond-shaped stone, different from the one he used to summon the crest and the filly. He reached over and pressed it into one of the man's wet hands.

"Can you use hands?" Dondio asked in the best English he could muster.

Just by having the stone against his flesh, the man seemed to gain new strength. An amount of cohesion joined his tone of voice.

"Yes," he said. "But my legs..."

"*Prendi!* Take this stone! It helps while I work."

The man did as Dondio bid, and soon the Strego's hands were waving over the injured body. It was an awkward way of doing things, as Dondio had never performed such a spell while lying on his side and trying to be as discrete as possible. The man's spasms raged on as Dondio worked first mending bones, then nerves and tissue. Since the spell was painful to the recipient, Dondio gave the man the small stone to hold. It was a different magic that made the torment of being healed nearly vanish.

Dondio finished repairing the man's spine and the vertebrae snapped back into natural shape with an audible *crack*.

The man let out a low groan but continued to hold the stone tightly. Dondio looked over to the guards. Only three were lined up at the side of the house where there had been five. Were they on patrol? Dondio's heart pounded harder at the thought. With sweat beading into his eyes, he began to work faster.

First, one leg cracked as the bones set back into place. Then the other snapped into shape. The man whimpered as the fingertips of both Dondio's hands touched his eyelids.

Dondio was hard at work when movement made him look up. The guards must have circled around the house, checking for intruders. Suddenly the guards raised their guns and charged right for him. Dondio sat up and drew his staff. The man on the ground moaned at the end of the healing sensation.

"Hold the stone," Dondio instructed. "Keep in the hand."

The man only twitched in response. The guards slowed as they closed in on him. They wore helmets low over their eyes, but Dondio suspected they could still see. This was proven true when one of the guards stopped and eyeless sockets regarded him from head to toe.

"The Mistress seeks a *Strego Bianco*," the guard said in Italian. "Are you he?"

The old Strego was taken aback that the guard spoke. If it was a reanimation spell the Strega Nera had used to assemble her guardsmen, as Dondio strongly suspected, then these men should be little more than shells, mere bodies to do physical labor. Years ago, he had read texts that were very clear as to what the spell could and could not do. Unless the Strega Nera had altered the spell somehow. Or tainted it with dark magic.

"It would please me to make your acquaintance first, good sir," Dondio replied in his most splendid northern-Italian dialect. "With whom do I have the pleasure of speaking?"

The guard's head tilted slightly, like a dog trying to process some confusing human action. "Are you he?"

Before he could answer, the other guard stepped over. He was a taller, more muscular man than the first, but both held the exact same posture.

"He is to be taken alive to the Mistress."

"Just what I was here for!" Dondio exclaimed. "It is very good that we passed each other out here. I was loath to knock."

As he stood, Dondio discretely pulled one of the many knives from his vest. In a flash he spun behind the unsuspecting guards. The two wheeled around quickly, but Dondio still had enough time to swing his staff at the head of the tall guard and drive his knife into the neck of the other.

The end of the staff crunched into the guard's head. The guard fell forward to the ground next to the nearly-healed American, who still twitched in his injury-induced stupor. His rifle bounced into the grass.

The attacker that Dondio had stabbed now wheeled around at him again, swinging the butt-end of the rifle with brutal force. It missed Dondio by centimeters but the guard followed up by driving the butt of the rifle into Dondio's gut. Dondio collapsed to the ground, burning to gain back his breath. The guard stomped over in two steps, reached down and snatched Dondio by the top of his hood. Instinctively, Dondio let his arms go limp and he leaned back. He slipped right out of his cloak and left the guard pondering the hood in his grip. With that extra moment, Dondio jabbed his staff forward from his low angle. The butt-end shattered the guard's kneecap and he toppled. Like a rivet-driver on the railroad, Dondio raised his staff high and brought the solid end down squarely on the unprotected back of the guard's head. The skull exploded into wet splatter.

No sooner did Dondio manage a decent breath, the soldier he had merely whacked with the staff grabbed his arms from behind. The grip was so deep into his arms that he cried out and dropped his staff. The guard's hands were gripped just above Dondio's elbows, and he clamped Dondio's arms with unnatural

strength that made movement impossible. Dondio was aston-
ished that the tall guard was able to recover so quickly. He hoped
the same would not be true for the guard with the smashed head.

He writhed about frantically, trying to loosen the clamp-like
grip of the guard. There was no hope in escaping. The Strega
Nera had managed to add a superhuman strength to the spells
she used on these men. The guard was careful to hold Dondio
as perfectly straight as possible, apparently concerned only with
following Mistress' orders. Without a word, the guard began
to trudge back to the house, with Dondio held before him in
straight arms, like a child being presented for baptism.

The tired Strego stopped struggling for a moment to think
over his options. The other three guards that stood at the side of
the house began to walk over to meet their comrade. Although
they also wore their helmets low, as if each of their heads were a
few sizes too small, the three approaching guards had no problem seeing the captive.

The blind faces looked at him in a manner that suggested
they didn't realize their eyes were covered. After a brief study,
the three guards relented and allowed Dondio and his captor to
pass. Red anger filled him as he tried to focus on an escape. He
could not reach his pouch, not with his arms pinned so tightly
to his sides. Even then, his spells might not work. This Strega
Nera was clever.

The muffled crack of gunshots startled him, and his captor stopped. The ground arrived suddenly and slammed into
Dondio's face. He felt warm blood from his nose, then the relief of his arms being freed. The weight of the guard that had
been carrying him bore down on his legs and he struggled to
turn around. When he realized the guard was not moving, he
scooted from under the body and surveyed the scene.

There was nothing around him. No movement, no guards
standing watch, no more gunshots. Dondio pawed the dirt and
grass from his eyes and mouth and looked around again. The

witch's guards were clumps on the ground, fallen right where they had stood. A few of them were collapsed at their posts near the house. He could only imagine what it signified.

"The magic of the Strega Nera has failed," Dondio said aloud. "That means she..."

He did not want to finish the sentence. Holding his nose, Dondio quickly dashed back to gather his staff. He would have to move quickly.

The American's condition had improved. He still gripped the stone tightly in his fist, and the spasms had ceased. After another survey of the land, Dondio went to his knees, no longer concerned with stealth. The man whined when the fingertips of Dondio's hands touched his eyelids. Dondio hushed him. With the man holding the stone, Dondio was able to amplify its power. Soon the man looked up at Dondio with clear eyes.

"Thank you," the man said flatly in English. "My legs work. I ain't twitching."

Dondio wiped fresh blood from his nose onto his arm. "Yes. Where is the Strega Nera?"

The stocky soldier sat in a silent daze that made Dondio want to reach out and shake him. Finally, the soldier looked up at Dondio. Even in the dark there was a bright gleam in his eye.

"I want to learn," the soldier said.

"*Che cosa?*"

"What you did," the soldier continued. "You healed me. Show me how."

Dondio stood with a huff and put his hands on his hips. "Soldier-man," he said. "What is your name?"

"Sam. Samson Arnold," the man said, rising to his feet. "Whatever you need, I'll do it. Just please, show me how to do what you did? It is a wonderful thing."

Dondio sighed heavily as he looked into the soldier's chubby face. "Sam, to learn takes time. Much time. I have hurry. Where is the Strega Nera?"

Some wonder left the soldier's face. "The witch?" he asked.
Dondio nodded.

Sam looked around, seeing the collapsed soldiers for the first time. "Haven't a clue," Sam said. "Tell you the truth, I haven't a clue what I seen in there. I've had to kill a man, and I seen a man turned into a dog, and I seen a witch talk to an owl, and now I seen you." He stared off. "No, I haven't a clue at all."

Dondio stood, one hand on his bearded chin, considering his options.

He untied the satchel at his belt, reached in, and grabbed another stone, then held the satchel out to Sam. The soldier took it carefully.

"You are not fully healed," Dondio said. "Magic only start healing process. You need rest. See that tree? The one split in two trees? Go north from tree. You find stream. Follow stream west until pond. At side North of pond, you will find a cave. Not a long walk. There you can rest and be safe. More stones in bag. Use them if you have hurt."

Sam listened closely. "And then," he said. "Will you meet me there?"

Dondio only gave him a flat gaze. "Young man, I do not know. I tell you, there are books in cave, hidden in rock. Books explain what you have in bag. Some in English. Study those until I return."

Sam beamed. "Thank you! Thank you, mister—"

"I am Strego Dondio Il Vecchio."

"Thank you, Stray-oh." Tears were welling in Sam's eyes.

"Go," Dondio said with a flick of his hand.

Sam nodded with a newly-resolute face and turned to go, clutching Dondio's satchel.

Dondio did not wait to see Sam off; he simply turned and began to walk toward the house. The wind felt good against his bare shoulders. Without his cloak and his satchel, he had a sense of buoyancy. With the feeling of lightness, his pride swelled with what he was about to do. Ever since the Lady spoke to him in his dreams and sent him on this journey, Dondio had been reacting to events around him, and in turn he always remained one step behind. Now he felt an intense urge to take control over something, to initiate action.

He hopped onto the porch without glancing at the two bodies on the ground. The door opened easily. A few oil lamps burned, which cast a dim, flickering light onto the immaculate decor. As quietly as he could, Dondio stepped around and shut the door. He wasted no time in pressing his palms to the door and letting his magic flow into it. He whispered some old words and tried to keep his leg from shaking through the strain of it all. When he was done he pulled his hands away and tried to open the door. It had been a long while since he had cast a shield spell, and he smiled when the door would not budge.

Just as he leaned back on his heels, the sound of footsteps approached. Dondio crouched low behind a chair.

"I can't believe those are the only cells," one of them, an American, said. "There have to be others."

"I say we bloody leave and be done with it," the other said, obviously an Englishman. "What can we do? Let's get some men and flatten this place."

"We have time now," the American said sternly. "The magic is gone. I'm going through every room in this cursed place."

"Well, I wish you luck then," the Englishman said, passing dangerously close to the place where Dondio crouched. The Englishman walked over to the front door and gave it a pull.

"Blasted door's jammed."

He gave it a few more tugs, and Dondio saw him put a boot to the wall and pull on the handle. He grunted as he pulled. The spell held strong and left the Englishman red in the face. On a small table near the entrance sat an arrangement of tea cups and saucers. The Englishman snatched one of the fancy saucers from the table and tossed it with all his might at one of the two windows to either side of the door. The porcelain dish shattered on the window without leaving a scratch. He then walked over to the window and pushed on it, with his hands flat on the glass. When that failed, the Englishman gave the door an angry kick and turned to the American.

"Not all the magic's failed," the Englishman said. "The doors and windows are bewitched. We can't get out of here. Go on, try it."

"I believe you," the American said in a tired voice. "C'mon."

The Brit gave the door one more spiteful look before turning to follow his companion. The two men disappeared into a doorway leading to another room. Dondio stole down the hallway through which the men had just come. About halfway down the carpeted hall was a heavy door which stood open. A burnt smell was in the air when he leaned in, and the hall was murky with smoke.

Dondio burst out running toward the source of the smoke.

CHAPTER 14

Differing Reflections

"I FEEL LIKE SOMEONE IS WATCHING us," Howard said, as they moved out of the kitchen and into another short hallway.

Ed grunted. The carpet was blue here and turned sharply to the right where there were stairs leading up. There were four small tables in the hallway, two at the entrance and two by the stairs. On each sat a trinket of some sort; one was a plate on a small mount, two were vases and another was an empty wooden bowl.

Howard eyed the items as well. His narrow face tightened as he focused on one of the vases. Casually, he flicked his wrist. With the back of his hand, Howard knocked the vase off the table. It hit the wall with a *thunk* and bounced to the carpet. Ed turned quickly at the sound, and then relaxed.

"Stop it," he told Howard. "That's not going to help."

"Seems I'm a klutz," Howard said. He walked over to the plate and knocked that to the floor as well. When it did not break either, he stomped his boot down on it and there was a muffled crunch.

Ed gave Howard a sour look.

"You can't expect me to be trapped in here and not smash something," Howard argued. "At least there'll be fewer dishes to do when she has her witch friends over for tea."

"She's dead," Ed reminded him. "She won't be wanting tea."

"Really?" Howard paused. "Sympathy for our captor?"

Ed turned and made his way up the steps. He heard the separate thuds of the other two items hitting the carpet behind him. Howard was muttering something to himself and Ed wondered if this place did indeed loosen things in a man's mind.

The top of the stairs opened to another hall. The floor was hardwood and the walls were a deeply-stained wood paneling. There was one door on either side, appearing to divide the upstairs in half with two rooms. Ed approached the one closest to him, the one on his left, and peered into the room. Its door stood half open, and Ed could feel the slight flow of air.

He nudged himself into the room and saw that it contained the huge window that he had seen when his patrol first arrived. It was shattered now and the night's cool breeze was strolling inside. The floor was scattered with wood chips and other debris Ed could not identify. A workbench of some sort was overturned and its contents of jars, tools and papers had spilled everywhere. Two large wooden tables sat in the middle of the room, tilted on one center leg at an angle to face the window. Ed's boots crunched over to a table and he noticed straps at the table's middle and at the bottom. He felt one of the straps with his fingers, and then winced with pain as the broken skin on his hand folded.

Howard issued a low whistle from across the room, and Ed walked over to him. A bookcase had toppled over, and behind that a naked man was curled into a ball. Howard and Ed exchanged a glance, and then Howard reached out with the butt of his rifle and pushed the man onto his back. He flopped over easily, a sign that he had not been dead long. Both men took a step back, and Ed gasped when the eyeless face of Corporal Clyde Wright came to view. It slowly rolled to the right, and then fell looking away, as if Wright would have nothing to do with them.

"That's one of my men," Ed finally managed to say. "Why did she...what did she do to him?"

"Looks like he had more fun than us," Howard said caustically.

Ed fought to control his sudden urge for violence. He faced Howard and moved in close enough to make both men feel uncomfortable.

"Give me a minute, soldier," Ed said through clenched teeth. His sharp blue eyes stared into the gray of Howard's for a moment more, and then he turned and took a knee next to his fallen countryman.

Howard lost the comical tightness of his face and now it slacked. He rocked self-consciously from foot to foot, and then seemed to realize it may be best to wait in the hall. Ed could hear the squeak of the floorboards as Howard paced outside the room.

Ed did not know why he told Howard he needed a minute. He was never a praying man, but he did sometimes feel as though there was something on his side, something looking over his shoulder. Wright's body seemed to lie in wait as Ed tried to conjure some good memories of him. There were good memories; Wright could be quite a character. Ed bowed his head. The prospect of finding his other two cohorts alive felt bleaker.

A few minutes later, Ed emerged. The hallway was empty and sounds of rummaging came from the room at the end of the hall.

"Good god," Howard said. "Look at this mirror!"

The ceiling of this room was slanted with the roof as well. It contained a great many more items than the previous room, and although its shelves and tables were stockpiled with all sorts of books and trinkets, figurines and powder-filled jars, it was an intensely organized chaos.

Ed saw the mirror standing against the wall, just right of the door. It had three sections of glass in it, and looked as if it were hinged so the sections could be folded up. The frame was molded to look like vines, in the most precise detail, complete with stems and leaves that bore a startlingly realistic texture. For a moment Ed thought he saw the silver vines moving, the leaves sliding against each other as they caught the candlelight. But it must have been a trick of the imagination. When he glanced into the mirror panes themselves, he saw the true wonder. Each pane reflected a different image.

It was natural to look forward, into the center mirror, so this is where Ed focused first. In the center he saw a reflected image of himself, or some version of himself, looking the same in face but drastically different in dress. The Ed in that mirror wore chain mail over his arms, chest, and legs, with a leather suit on top of that. Instead of a gun in his hand, this Ed held a long sword and a shield strapped to his back. A leather strap around his waist held an ax in place and his hands wore metal gauntlets that glistened with the fire of a torch mounted on the stone wall behind him. The man who looked like Ed seemed noble yet harsh, cruel yet fair. Ed felt diminished in comparison with his green army clothes.

His eye was drawn then to the mirror on the right. This one was even more outrageous. It was himself again, the reflection following Ed's every movement. The reflection had long hair, dyed red and pulled back tight to the back of his skull. He wore an open red vest that showed a physique much more developed than Ed expected. War paint had been drawn on the skin, reminding Ed of cowboy and Indian games he once played as a child. A horizontal black stripe of paint went across the eyes and down the sides of the neck. On his chest, symbols were drawn that Ed could not make out. He saw a woman sitting cross-legged in the background, gazing at Ed with a look of understanding. The woman had red hair as well, and her breasts were exposed, but she sat with the regal authority and dignity of a queen.

The mirror on the left looked as close to his expectations as possible. The reflection was his own, in the same room, but as he looked more closely, he saw there were some notable differences. His gun was the first difference he could see. The one in the reflection was smaller, sleeker and newer looking. It had a strange flashing green light on it, and it was equipped with a scope that looked like nothing more than a mounted square of glass. He noticed with great surprise that instead of having USA stamped on his left breast, the Ed in this mirror had USR. He couldn't imagine what that meant.

"Oh!" Howard suddenly popped up behind him. "My estate has a triptych similar to this, although much finer in craftsmanship," Howard paused. "How come you show up in that frame, and I don't?"

Ed could see Howard in the first two mirrors; the first reflection showed him standing next to Ed in armor, the second showed them both wearing the same strange red get-up with the war paint, but in the third reflection, Ed stood alone, no Howard whatsoever. Howard waved his hand in front of Ed, but that one mirror still reflected only Ed's image.

"They're different worlds," Ed said in a soft, awed voice.

"And I suppose I don't exist in that one," Howard said with spite. He raised his chin at the mirror in contempt. "Fine, I don't mind, I didn't care to exist in that world, anyhow."

"We need to stop playing," Ed said, finally breaking his attention from the mirrors. Interesting as they were, he had the lives of two fellow soldiers to think about, not to mention the lives of Howard and himself.

Howard scoffed at him. "Playing? We're investigating. We'll unravel this quagmire and be back at camp eating cheese and government issued sausages in no time. Not the sort of sausages you would prefer, I'm sure. We'll have to ride out to Florence or Milan and scope out the bathhouses for something like that."

Ed turned away, his eyes darting around the room for some sign of his men. Would he see the metals from their uniforms among the small, glittering tokens? Ed saw a candy dish on a small end-table and the thought of food, even a small amount of food, sent his stomach into a roar. He lifted the glass lid carefully and saw nothing worth eating. Inside were several shriveled little items that might have once been candy, years ago. They were dried out, translucent yellow and cracked with age, perhaps sugar balls of some sort. He wondered how often Inara had hosted mutually agreeable company.

There was a door on one wall. It was a closet, just as Ed had suspected. He continued to walk around the room and saw no trace of Arnold or Oaks among the miscellaneous trinkets. Ed had the strong feeling that each item did serve a purpose that he was too unskilled to see. Ed sighed and pinched the top of his nose between two tightly shut eyes.

Howard whistled at something and made an exclamation, but Ed was not listening. He felt a wave of despair. He knew he should not feel bad about killing the witch, she was his captor after all, but something about it did not seem right. He felt as if he had made a huge mistake. The guilt of destroying some priceless piece of art or irreplaceable treasure made his heart heavy and head hang low. He hadn't been able to look at her body after he did it. Could he tell anyone what he'd done, even under the circumstances? Could he tell Beth? Could he look into her hazel eyes, eyes that weren't so different in shape from Inara's, knowing what he'd done? And he hit her from behind too, a coward's attack. When Ed was younger, he used to pretend to be a cowboy. Billy The Kid was his favorite, and he'd run around his neighborhood hooting and hollering and firing caps. He hated the story of Billy The Kid's death. A relentless sheriff, whom Ed always pictured being draped in shadow, appeared behind Billy just as he walked into a room and blew his brains out. Ed felt sick to his stomach.

"They aren't here. Let's go," he called to Howard. He looked over to see the Englishman staring into a box and making no move to respond. Ed walked over and saw the man's eyes were wide, with tears forming, his gaze unmoving and intensely focused on one thing. Huge wet drops stormed down his rough cheeks and Ed waited for him to blink, but he never did. Howard had the box sitting on one of the over-packed tables, having scooted a number of different items aside. His hands gripped the edge of the table so hard his knuckles were white.

Ed waved his hands in front of Howard's face and said his name a few times, each time louder than the last.

"Stop fucking with me," Ed told him. "We have to go. Come on!"

Howard seemed oblivious.

Frustration overwhelmed Ed and he grabbed the inside of Howard's elbow and tugged. He almost stumbled backward when the man remained stone still. Ed balanced himself and then tugged again, more forcefully. Still, as if a statue weighted with tons of concrete, Howard did not budge.

CHAPTER 15

Aradia's Crest

DONDIO PRESSED HIS FOREHEAD TO Inara's. Her skin was dead cold. Despite all, his waning power seeped into her, feeling and clawing until it gripped upon what little was still there. Trying to veil both his panic and joy, he spoke to her.

"I cannot heal you, Strega."

"*Good.*"

"You must help. I am weakened and can only do so much."

"*No. I am dead.*"

"You are close, but not yet. That spark still flickers in your spine, that spark that is you, the true you, unmolested by the choking black shadow, the smoke and vapor of Malocchio."

"*I don't care.*"

Dondio became aware of the cold stone of the chamber under his feet and wished he were outdoors, planted firmly in the Earth's soil where he could draw from the Lady's energy. So much of his own power had been spent on healing the broken-back American that even contact with the Earth herself might not be enough.

"Damn the rot of Malocchio," he said, and grunted as he picked up Inara in his arms. He cupped her head as gently as he could, feeling tangled clumps of hair damp with blood. Quickly, he made his way down the dimly lit hallway.

Was it those two soldiers that had done this to her? Justified or not, Dondio swore under his breath that he would tear the flesh from their bones, bit by bit, if his daughter did not survive. A daughter rediscovered only to be lost – was that the bounty of Aradia? Had he traveled so long at the Lady's bequest for this?! Under how many different suns had he waged battled? How many worlds had he spent lifetimes trying to correct?

Embrace me and damn me both, Lady of Life. Strangle me till my throat is but a reed, enough air to stay alive but not be alive. I am Aradia's crest, to be ripped in two by talons before being devoured. After time and trials indefinite, put a daughter in my arms, but first crack her skull like an eggshell, spill her blood over my arms, and keep those eyes closed with death so that Elisa's green gaze forever remains the memory it has long been. I've never asked of you, Lady, never, but this ... it is too much and too cruel. Any Strego other than me could have done this, could have served you here. Yet you summoned me, and how I trusted your direction, fool I am.

"Perhaps I summoned you with purpose, Dondio."

The old Strego nearly dropped his ward from his arms, flicking his gaze madly around the dim hall until he saw Her. A small woman, pale and young in face, wearing simple peasant's garb of a plain dress and hood covering a head of red curls. She spoke in ancient Etruscan, and She smiled at him knowingly.

"Curse you, Aradia!" Dondio spat. "Come You to see me at my worst? In my grief? Have You some new punishment for me or for my dead daughter?"

Aradia's expression did not change on Her pale face. She took steps toward him. His back touched the stone wall before he knew he was backing up, and he hissed cruel words at Her in the Old Tongue, words he hoped would scorn Her heart as She had scorned his. Still Her face remained in a calm smile, Her beauty all the more apparent as She came closer. Her lips curved in a familiar way under a nose peppered lightly with freckles and then he truly saw Her eyes, the beautiful green of life.

Her pale hand reached out to him, and he felt the urge to attack it though he did not want to release his grip on his daughter. The hand reached to his chest, through the hair of his beard, and with no place to go he flattened himself further against the wall. The hand tugged away suddenly, and She took something from around his neck. Giaccomo's necklace. The white orb pendant. Aradia stepped away to reveal the charm hanging between Her fingers. There was almost instant relief for Dondio.

"Malocchio's taint is like venom in the blood," She said in a voice that, without Malocchio's fouled pendant at his breast, was now a beautiful song. "Can you not feel it, Dondio?"

He realized he had felt the taint, realized it only because it was now gone. It had soaked into his soul so fast. Why had he worn the pendant?!

"Malocchio threatens this world, though I doubt he even knows it. The Evil Eye must not leave this house."

His hands wobbled under Inara's form, but his lips suddenly tightened, and he looked at Aradia with a gaze as straight as when sighting his bow.

"Is this how You do it then?" he asked Her plainly, voice nearly a whisper. "All of You deities, from Jupiter to the Jade Emperor to Jesu, do You lead us mortals along, offering or refusing aid upon whim?"

Her smile never left, but Her head tilted slightly down, and in that gesture was all the empathy and understanding that could fill a tome of words. She held the pendant out to him, cord entwined in Her fingers, as if offering it back. Abruptly the glass-enclosed eye burst into blue flames. The blue tongues of fire licked Her fingers as they snaked up the cord until the pendant was nothing more than flakes of ashes fluttering to the floor.

"Heal her," Dondio said coldly. "You may have removed Malocchio's taint from me, but I'll still curse You if You let my daughter die."

Aradia gave a chuckle. "Always the same with you, Dondio. Defiant in the end, after a lifetime of loyalty."

Aradia's hand darted out and clasped Dondio's arm, halting his movement. The dark hallway brightened, and Inara now lay at his feet. Had he dropped her?

"No," Aradia said. "I placed her there. Do not worry, Dondio."

"It's what I do," Dondio said. "I wander the world, and I worry."

"Aye, it's true," Aradia laughed again. "And what I do, Strego Bianco, is come to you in your most precarious times of need."

"Come to me? How?"

"You never remember," she went on. "But I'm always there. You are My extraordinary creature, Dondio. Mine and the Mother Diana's. If there is help to be given, it is yours. It's always yours, Great Guardian."

A surging of memories entered into his consciousness and Dondio remembered it all. He remembered the first time, taking an arrow clean through the throat during the storming of the lost-to-history City of Nior. The second time, a cave-in crushed him to death while working as a Welsh slave in a Roman gold mine. The third time his boat capsized while trying to fend off the Normans. It went on, and he remembered every time, and as his memories unfolded he remembered going further and further into realms of existence, meeting ends there, always with the same result. Every time She came. Every time, She was there to cup his torn throat in her hands and somehow piece his flesh together, to brush Her hand over the bolder that

almost crushed him and crumble it to sand, to offer him a hand
to the surface just as his lungs were about to fill with water.

Now his arm burned where Her hand clutched him, and he
felt like a fool for berating Her.

"No, not a fool," She said soothingly, his thoughts apparently as clear to Her as a brightly painted sign. "That is what
makes you *you*. It is why We value you so. That is why you must
never know."

"But I know now," he said.

"There is always the random," Aradia went on. "Always the
unexpected. A heart valve could burst. Debris from the heavens
could fall and crush you. The wind could blow a little creature,
so small you could not even see it, into your lungs where it could
plant itself and infect you unto death. But if I can, I'll be here
to offer you aid."

He felt Her grip tighten on his arm, but Her hands were
now holding a mass of fur, a rat. She took it by the tail, where
it dangled until the fingers of Her free hand pinched into the
rodent's soft belly. Her hand grew dark as She worked, and soon
She pulled a bloodied rock from the innards.

"The *larè* swallowed it when he realized who I was," She said.
"As if that would help." The moonstone bounced to the ground.
The rat, just as Giaccomo's pendant, curled and burned in Her
hands, smoldering and smoking as it curled into ash, dark soot
falling from between Her long, pale fingers.

"You cannot know," Aradia said, looking at Dondio. "Because
knowing would change you. You cannot know I will shield you
from destruction. You cannot know of the guardian looking
over your shoulder. Even passive knowledge of My protection
would manipulate the outcome of your actions."

"Curse the games of the gods," Dondio said.

Aradia smiled, bold and beautiful. "Always the same, my
sweet, loyal Dondio. No matter the time, the place, the world,
it is always you. Now save your daughter. She is needed as well."

Aradia entwined Her fingers and let sway both hands until they rippled like a gentle pond. They rose and fell, along with Dondio's eyes as he watched. He heard the lap of water and the caws of seabirds. Dondio felt sudden sailor's leg and reached back for purchase, vision blurred and thoughts unclear.

Dondio steadied himself and saw Inara on the ground. Had he dropped her? He thought he might have felt faint a moment ago. How had Inara gotten to the floor? Perhaps the healing of the American had weakened him more than he realized. As he put a hand to her cold forehead, Dondio felt the power of healing surge through him. He wondered how his power, so recently drained, had returned. But that did not stop him from taking advantage and letting the energy flow from him into her.

His power felt stronger than it ever had, and rather than allow himself to be dumbfounded by this unexpected resurgence, he focused harder. He felt her tissues restore, felt her brain reawaken and begin its tasks once more as if nothing had ever stopped.

"*Who are you?*" Inara asked, in a voice that came from deep within her spine, resonating more as a hum than as human words.

"A priest," he said.

He held her, his daughter. She had the same forehead, the same ears, only smaller. Her chin was Elisa's, and he recognized the height of the nose with respect to the cheekbones. And the eyes, of course. The most beautiful aspects of her mother melded with his. The pleasingly wide set of her eyes, her soft lips, her straight nose and high cheekbones.

He let go of her and sat, taking a spot next to her on the cold stone floor. He'd done all he could, and it was in the hands of The Lady now. Dondio was tired, too. He shifted in place and felt a rock underneath, poking into his buttocks. Reaching for it, he felt its smooth surface and its cold temperature. He held it up. In the dim light the stone had an opaque green color, and he knew it for what it was.

"Moonstone shard," Inara said, sitting up. "Careful not to look into it, old man."

But he already had. He had looked into it and saw nothing but the churning of swamp-colored clouds.

"Don't, you fool!" Inara said more forcefully. "It's there I've captured Malocchio. I can tell you are powerful, but don't tempt fate and give him means of escape."

"It seems he's found the means," Dondio said. He looked at her squarely. "You *captured* the Evil Eye?"

"Yes, he's right there in the moonstone."

"It's empty," he said, handing her the moonstone. Her beautiful green eyes widened in surprise. As she grasped it, her hand was shaking.

"Gone? Where is he? What happened?"

Dondio regarded her frankly. "You were hurt, and it seems your power failed. Your…guardsmen crumpled to the ground just before I found you."

"And you healed me, priest?"

He said simply, "Yes."

Inara looked at Dondio. Gods, they were the eyes he remembered. *Thank you, Lady of Life, for allowing me to see them again.* He struggled to keep his composure.

"You do not serve him, then. Malocchio?" Dondio asked.

"I served him unto a prison cell," Inara said. "He will be coming for me."

"That he will," said Dondio. "Do this: keep the empty moonstone, and say these words: *Fluisca il sangue del nemico. Illumina la pietra dell'eternità.*"

Inara held the empty moonstone in her open palm. "Why?"

"Because you have a choice. Bianco and Nero. When you look at yourself in the mirror, you have a choice. Repeat the words to me."

"*Fluisca il sangue del nemico. Illumina la pietra dell'eternità,*" she said.

"Good," said Dondio, who could not hide his smile.

"American Edward!" Inara gasped. "By the Gods, Malocchio cannot have him!"

Dondio saw in her face the fear that was rising in his heart. "Well, come!" he said, grabbing her wrist. She stuffed the empty moonstone into her pocket and together they ran for the stone doorway that led back into the farmhouse. Before they could get there, a guard with empty eye sockets appeared in front of them, then another. Dondio's bare feet skidded to a halt, Inara just short of crashing into him. Two more guards shuffled in behind the first, then two more.

"Slaves," Inara called out. Her voice assumed such a potent tone of command, Dondio looked at her in surprise. "I want every room searched and American Edward captured. *Pronto!*"

The guards made no move to obey, rather they remained where they were, a wall of bodies blocking the doorway.

Inara stepped in front of Dondio, irritation carried on her pointed shoulders.

"*Slaves!*" she said again, with even more commanding force. "Stand down, so says your Mistress."

Instead their rifles rose as they took aim. The two nearest them, the first two to block the door, spoke in unison with sagging jaws and gurgled voices. "There is no mistress," they said. "There is only Lord Malocchio."

Gunfire erupted.

CHAPTER 16

Malocchio

HELLO, HOWARD. NOW THAT WE share a body, I think it wise that we get to know each other. But I suppose I owe you a bit of honesty. What I meant to say was that I think it wise that you get to know *me*.

Someday I will document this story. It will be the sacred text which my cult reveres and for which they kill. *The Many Martyrdoms of Malocchio* I may call it, or *Rebirth Annointed in Rue*. I require a title that mocks the gods.

During my ten years confined within the bitch's moonstone, I died thousands of times. Sometimes I died twice in one day. This new life, this human *flesh*, has restored my appreciation. Ah, to be a man again. I've lost and regained the flesh before, but the time inside that stone, the *deaths* I endured, make this new form all the more pleasing. A man's body, finally! How tired I was of birds, moths and ants (especially ants; rather the gods damn me to the Veil than to have another life as an ant).

Your body runs heavy with the blood of the Normans, I am pleased to say. I was born to a mother with such blood-ties, but that particular body (my first and the one for which I am most nostalgic) was wrapped in vines, annointed with rue branches, twined with silver, and burned. I escaped that body before the burning and was in fact one of the men who tightened the vine whips around my own ankles.

Each death lingers, phantom agonies where memory persists, the painful tingle of a long-severed limb. How it enrages me! Were the bitch not dead (and she must be dead, if I am free, she must be) I would rake her body and soul with pain and sorrow. Out of spite, I would keep her living a long while to suffer the most profound and profane of invasions I could contrive. In death, Inara made an easy escape.

My time in the moonstone was not without hope. The bitch had caught me, I knew it immediately. My own power sealed me in. Her strength was in reflection and timing. My own power doubled over and stifled me. I was subdued and humiliated, but—as the little bitch knew—I was not defeated. She only had to relax the slightest amount of strength, and I would expand like a coiled spring. Still, I would need a suitable vessel, a body to possess.

I do not know what happened to my human form when the little bitch trapped me. It was my one-hundred and seventy-ninth human body. I had been enjoying myself at a brand-new French hotel on the Vietnamese coast. Pia was always too prompt, stuck as she was in the old ways, and contacted me at High Midnight sun. I was in bed with the corpses of two prostitutes I had acquired earlier that week. Most certainly unprepared for an attack, I leaned away from the room and into the depths of the moonstone to answer her. Minutes later, Pia was dead and I was suffocating inside a crystalline prison.

My hope arrived after my initial retaliation. I lashed out in rage and shattered the moonstone in which I was trapped. The little bitch gathered all the pieces she could, severely limiting my chances of escape, but she could not find them all. Luck was with me, for within hours after my capture, a finch caught the glare of one of the shards and carried it back to its nest. I could not escape into animals, but I could bring them under my control. *Larè* is the old word for that. With a bit more luck, I hoped that I could use a *larè* to lure a human to look into the stone. Then I would be free. My theory could not be tested, though, as the finch did not look deep into the moonstone it carried; it simply grasped the stone with its talons and deposited it into the nest. While the stone sat useless within an old sycamore tree, other shards were revealed that Inara had missed. I took control of an owl, a centipede, a moth, a rat. The bitch was thorough and had anticipated this, and each of my *larè* were eaten or smashed to bits before I could truly use them to my advantage. As her collection of shards grew, my hope for escape dwindled.

The finch that dropped my stone into its nest never returned (hence the irony of my initial optimism) and I cannot speculate as to what happened to it. The stone remained there for years as I pursued other means of escape, but never did I forget where that stone lay.

A few years passed before a common worker ant happened to crawl into the nest and, unintentionally, glanced into the murky depths of the moonstone. Thus began my many deaths, as if one hundred and seventy-nine were not already enough. The ant became mine, and I pushed the creature's kernel of willpower to the side. It was much less enjoyable than possessing you, Howard.

Cruelly limited, I had only enough power to ensnare one creature at a time, so her fellow ants that arrived with her did me more harm than good. I broke rank with the scavenging team, and began emitting my scent, which would inform the colony that abundant food existed in the abandoned bird's nest. The ants that were with me quickly saw the mendacity of my communique, and judging me injured or mad, they surrounded my ant body and portioned me to bits with their tiny jaws. My first death as an ant, and not nearly the most painful.

Regardless of the ants' suspicions, the call for food was strong. Within days, a stream of ants made a steady pilgrimage to the long-abandoned nest. I now had an endless supply of *larè*, who released more of that compelling scent at my behest. For all that, it did little to remove the stone, for each time I controlled a *larè* and tried to break away from the main strength of the ants, the dutiful drones executed me post haste. In this way I suffered many deaths. Once during a torrential rainstorm, a *larè* of mine managed to work its way down the sycamore's truck, where I hid under some bark and foolishly became cemented in sap. I struggled over-zealously until I tore off my own legs and remained in agony until I starved. Another time I survived all the way to the forest floor, where I was accosted by a strange red beetle with a horn on its head. It reared its legs at me and sprayed a poison that burned so severely, I questioned whether I felt it through human nerves or the simple sensations of ants.

Each death I recall in explicit detail. I suffered three such deaths at the jaws of a centipede. I discovered the beast's lair a few branches below the nest, and tried twice to lure it up, and twice it devoured me. My trial and error provided me with a plan, however. On the third attempt I successfully lured it into the nest, where it found the insect equivalent of a feast. It ate me, along with many of my comrades, and was given almost no choice but to look into the moonstone, for I had sprayed the smooth surface with ant scent and it was covered with their dark bodies. Once the centipede was my *larè*, I gave my rage to the ants, which had stifled me so. I made a day of tearing through their ranks. Then my operation became more delicate, as I knew I had to make the most of the opportunity.

But the centipede, I realized, was sick, which explains why it was hidden in its lair until I disturbed it. Its thorax was dotted with sensitive bumps that were sore and wept yellow ooze as I traversed the branches. It died before I got out of the tree.

I captured dozens more insects, and I had dozens more failures. All while the bitch peered into the moonstone to taunt me. It was not until I finally managed to capture a young dove that I saw how far she had taken the dark magic. In my glee at capturing a bird, I flew to get an outside view of the house, even before grabbing the moonstone from the nest. That's when I saw them. *Bal taek bhan.* The Nameless Ones, lined up in a protective perimeter around her lair.

How I laughed that day! She was a Strega Nera and didn't even know it! She used my magic and yet thought herself free. Ah, the corruptive properties of my very presence! It was very pleasing. I laughed so hard; my *larè*'s gizzard ruptured and choked me to death in mid-flight. But that death was worth it. I knew then the bitch's moon was waning. I almost laughed again when, as my owl, I saw the Strego Bianco stalking outside.

I'm laughing now, too, and this other soldier is staring at me, calling me your name in that ugly bastardized Anglo language. Howard, he wants to know if you're well. But you are not. You are more imprisoned now than when you were chained to the wall with your pants down.

"Gael," I say to him, and he looks at me with stupid confusion. Condensation on my skin! Human perspiration! "It is good to be alive, is it not?"

"Put the box down!" he shouts at me in that ugly, modern language. The fool is still concerned with the moonstone box. Useless trinket, now. I toss it over my shoulder and hear it ricochet and break some other of the Strega's nonsense playthings. He looks after it dumbly. Gaels understand nothing more than what their eyes present to them. They are peaches to be plucked, skinned, and devoured.

I turn and look at him. He must see something in my face he does not like because his gun is raised and pointed at me now. Why must he be here? I wish to enjoy your body for a while, Howard. To enjoy my reverie, so much more pleasant with a human brain at my command. The lower animal and insect brains took their toll on me, in the way that looking into the sun day after day blinds a man. The ease of thinking human thoughts! And the fool Gael keeps talking, interrupting.

Before I destroy the Gael and harvest his life's blood for mine own purposes, I speak the words and spiral the magic out and around, in and underneath the house, a cylindrical spell I penned myself. I speak to my slaves in my native tongue. Etruscan, they call it now, but I prefer the old name, *our* name. I tell them: *"Friends! Hear your true Lord Malocchio. Your Mistress is but soot on the bare soles of a whore."* This was an old Etruscan saying. The magic agrees well with the ancient proverbs. Their loyalty assured, I say: *"Scour these grounds, Nameless Ones. Destroy anyone your false Mistress had harbored."*

I am standing with my hands raised, seemingly staring at the wall, and the Gael looks lost as to what to do. I begin speaking to him, forgetting myself and using Etruscan words that he would find to be indecipherable. His face gets even more confused and I cannot help but laugh. So I laugh and laugh. How good it feels!

"Who are you?" the Gael asks me in American English, his eyes following my disfigured hand as I toss aside the moonstone that was my prison.

He has deduced that you, Howard, are not yourself. And he is correct. It was your folly to gaze into the moonstone.

As I answer him, I begin the painful process of rearranging my structure. Human pain is so much sweeter than that of the lower creatures. So many more synapses in the human brain to interpret pain. Short of being burned alive, pain is a wonderful equalizer between thought and action, astral and physical. The first sensation I perceived in this new body was a slap on the face, and with its sting I knew I was home in flesh. My face is molding to my design, that sentimental figure of my birth, so easily overriding the blueprint of my host. Bones shift, snapping and fusing, turning like gears under my skin. My features are fluid, clumping and churning into my true face.

"I am Malocchio. I am he who was annointed with rue and silver and burned," I say out loud, my speech skewed by the repositioning of joints in my jaw. Anger fills me as my spine cracks and grows taller. "He who was burned by the Streghi Bianchi. Those very same Streghi who would use you, Gael."

"Why did they burn you?" the Gael asks.

"For philosophy," I tell him in truth. I laugh and some old teeth clatter to the ground, having been replaced. "For fear. They burned a man with no violence in his heart, no anger, no malice. Only a desire to contribute to history, to participate in world events. A man must leave his mark."

The Gael eyes pay me heed, but that rifle of his remains solidly aimed at my head. What beautiful pain that fire-stick would bring. I almost want him to put a bullet in me, but not yet. Let my flesh reconfigure, then there will be the bloodletting pain of wounds, for myself and for him and for others, in blessed equality.

"A mark, or a stain?" the Gael asks me. Mincing words; a politician's ruse I have little taste for.

"A ripple," I counter. "Whatever the cause, wherever the ripples may travel, it is enough to know it was I who tossed the stone. Who am I, you ignorant time-misplaced Gael? I am the blind rage of the unjustly punished, the all-seeing tranquility in those over-wrought with sloth. I am contradiction, man without body, soul without god, the blinded cyclopean eye that sees more astutely than all the eyes on this earth."

Those were to be my last words to the Gael before I brained him, but the sound of shots garnered the attention of us both.

Below, my loyal slaves are cleaning house. The Gael darts for the door. I instinctively pursue, but in my haste I forget that my body is still changing. One leg is not quite the same size or shape as the other, and my first step tosses me to the floor. I hear my right femur snap under my weight. I will be fine in a few moments, and the pain is good.

I am curious as to what the slaves have killed, and concerned over the Strego Bianco who is surely afoot. Perhaps I underestimated their usefulness. I realize the Gael's potential. His blood could be mated with any one of my Streghe on this earth, and their strong and powerful fruit could be mine. Yes, a fine body that would make for Lord Malocchio. Sorry Howard, but I'm already in the market for your replacement.

CHAPTER 17

The Great Guardians

TWO SOLDIERS HELD THEIR RIfleS as Ed charged down the hallway toward them. Ed had no intention of stopping. *Shoot*, he thought. *Better to die by bullets than by magic of demons.* The pair of soldiers raised two dark barrels and aimed straight at Ed. But something was strange; their flesh dripped and sagged.

When the shots rang out, Ed was certain he had been hit. The dual flashes of the blasts burned in his vision. He waited for the pain to erupt somewhere on his body and for the inevitable follow-up shots.

But the pain did not come, he was not injured. Ed slowed his charge, cautiously approaching the two soldiers, who now leaned into one another like a house of cards. Dark bullet holes smoked in the floor at their boots.

As the smoke of gunfire dissipated, the repugnant odor of decay hit Ed. The rifles were down at the soldiers' feet, lying in a mush that could have been the sol-diers' fingers. One soldier took a step toward Ed, but the leg buckled before it gained a second lopsided knee. The soldier hit the ground hard and burst like an over-ripe melon. The ampli-fied stench made Ed gag.

The companion teetered wildly toward Ed. *No eyes*, Ed thought as the helmet bounced off. Waving a rotted stump of an arm as if it was still whole, the eyeless soldier made an inhu-man lunge in Ed's direction. The effort was as fruitless as before. Ankle crumbling as if made of cheap plaster, the soldier col-lapsed at Ed's boots, not bursting like the other but not moving again either.

The smell made Ed hack as he stepped over the dead. But he froze in silence when he heard boots clanking up the steps. Without thinking he slipped into the other room where he and Howard had found Wright's sprawled body. Ed shut the door silently behind him. *Fool*, he thought. *A lot of good this will do.*

The shattered window let in the night breeze that carried a bite of cold. His uniform clung uncomfortably to his skin from all his sweat and he shivered while he looked out the window. Instinct told him the best thing would be to hurl himself out that window and be done with it before the de-mon or monster or whatever it was could get to him. But then there would be no one left to stop it. The image of Inara's corpse flashed in his memory.

Just as he was turning from the window, something solid slammed into him and knocked him back. He tottered in the open air, and only his quickly placed hand saved him from plummeting. Pain erupted in his hand as his wound reopened, the thing that crashed into him writhing wildly in violent jerks.

It was a dog, a horrible dog with no eyes and gnashing jaws that bit into his arm. Already the bulk of meat on his left fore-arm was gone, and the creature's teeth were clamping on bare bone. Ed's legs wobbled, and he fell to a knee, but he managed to use his mangled arm as a shield. The dog was in a blind frenzy, biting at the air until it found its home on Ed's arm.

Ed found himself against the wall, the open window to his immediate left like a vacuum, pulling cold air past him in a constant rush of wind. He had the thought to drag the creature to the window and try to shove it out, but he feared if he tried that he would go over the edge as well. Still, it was all he had. He braced himself on the wall and lunged forward at the gnawing and clawing dog. The beast's hind legs buckled, then it stumbled backward, free from Ed's forearm, taking with it the last bit of dangling flesh. Ed had but a moment to breathe before the beast rebounded and clamped down on the arm again. Ed stabbed forward down the dog's neck, with the jagged bone that was his arm. A guttural yelp came from the dog, a squeal of surprised pain. It tottered a moment before falling to the side, and Ed fell backward to the floor.

Except he wasn't on the floor. He felt air. In stomach-dropping realization, he knew.

I fell out the window.

The impact never came. Air around him pillowed into supportive waves, and he felt a comfort he hadn't felt since before he crossed The Pond to fight the Nazis. His arm was gone; at least he thought so because he couldn't feel it. Or see it.

But he could see *something*. A face, maybe? Yes, it was a face, as if forming from liquid to solid.

The witch!

"No," a deep male voice spoke. "I am Dondio, servant of the Lady of Life. And the witch is Strega Inara. But that does not make her your enemy."

The face of a woman was coming into focus, next to the bearded form of Dondio.

What do you want?

"For you to live."

He felt fine, though he found he couldn't move. The room was coming back into focus as well, the bearded man and little woman standing unassumingly amid the wreckage.

"Gods and men are at war," she said. "Not just here, but everywhere."

I've had my share of the war.

The old man laughed. "I have fulfilled my duty and my service. It is you, Edward Layne, who will relieve me. A new Guardian, for a new time."

But I'm dying.

Dondio chuckled. "You are not dying. You are being saved."

Ed had to blink. When his eyes opened, the witch named Inara was standing over him. He squeezed what he thought was his injured hand, only to find it was free of pain. In his palm was a round stone.

"I have need of help," Inara said. "I cannot do alone."

Ed closed his eyes once more, convinced he was caught in the hallucinations of death. Perhaps if he blinked enough his Elizabeth would appear before him. Ed wished to think of her as he passed.

"You must help each other," the bearded man murmured to Inara.

"WHAT IS THIS?" another deep voice boomed.

Ed saw a tall, angular man. It was still Howard's clothes the man wore, though his wrists and ankles extended far past the uniform's limits. The man's long, sharp features regarded Ed accusingly. "Nameless Ones! To me!"

Ed felt the words reverberate through his bones and he wondered if they emanated in shock waves from a grenade blast.

"So good to see you again, Strega Nera," the strange, tall man said. "I'm glad you survived the attack so that I might have the opportunity to kill you myself. And Dondio! A true gathering, this is! A witch-whore, a Celtic lord, bitch Aradia's favorite Strego Bianco, and the greatest Strego Nero there ever was.

Why, we could have a true circle and sing the Elder songs and take turns fucking the whore to death! I know I plan to, and then some after. It's always better when they're cold." Slyly, he looked at Ed and winked.

Ed saw the man called Dondio; a scrawny old hermit, by his looks, with a long gray beard and even longer hair. The man wore a ragtag arrangement of clothes and carried a powerful wooden staff strapped to his back.

"Always a prisoner of desire, Malocchio," said the hermit. "The true great divide between Bianco and Nero always was the difference between what the individual wants and what the Lady of Life wants. Yours is a life too long and too wasted, squandered on striving to satisfy animal desires and attain heavenly powers."

Dondio stepped aside from the door, his arm outstretched. Inara stepped next to him, dancing in her steps as she darted from the room. Ed truly saw her now, innocent and beautiful. How could he ever, *ever* have thought she was a whore?

"*Whore!*" growled Malocchio. "Get back here!"

The air around Ed's head crackled and hissed. As Malocchio charged after her, Ed rose to his feet on reflex, anger heating his blood. He lunged to grab the demon but only caught the empty air. Malocchio was gone.

Ed's own exit from the room was stopped by a wooden staff that shot out across the doorway. The man named Dondio stood there, regarding him with sharp eyes, eyes younger than the man wearing them.

"She must lure the demon," Dondio said. "It's our only hope of trapping him again."

The march of footsteps could be heard coming up the stairs.

"Lure him where?" Ed asked, still gathering his bearings.

"You will see," Dondio said, grabbing Ed's shoulder. "I will deal with the demon's guards. But you have more important job. *Protect* her. When the vines extend, grab onto her and hold on for dear life!"

"Vines?"

"*Obey!* Go to Inara! You will know it when you see it!"

Ed had served in the military long enough to know the tone of command. Dondio removed his staff, and Ed burst into the hallway just as the first of the eyeless soldiers cleared the stairs.

Ed glanced back to see the old hermit spinning his staff at the soldiers and speaking odd words, words that may have been Italian or some other foreign language.

Ed found Inara standing in front of her tri-fold mirror, that strange thing trimmed in cast-metal vines that resembled a three-paneled, moving-picture screen. He felt the urge to go to her, Dondio's words still echoing in his ears. *Protect her.* He darted to her, heedless of the demon between them.

CHAPTER 18

Dogs and Men

REYNOLDS HAD SPENT THE NIGHT fighting. Beastly dogs, eyeless soldiers. There were periods of time in which his guns did not function, and then suddenly fired again. But lord, when they worked, he used them. Something was happening inside that house, especially when all those eyeless soldiers rose up and began to file back in like it was opening day at Wrigley. Reynolds had been able to hide, to pick off threatening creatures when he could, and he was tired.

Alone, Reynolds resolved to storm the house, and find shelter. All the men under his command were dead, so the way he saw it, he was on borrowed time anyway. Nonetheless, that didn't mean Sargeant Leopold Reynolds would lie down and die.

With every step, Reynolds expected to be ambushed. His head on a swivel, he scanned the horizon. The house was four hundred yards in front of him, with minimal ground cover. To his left, a thicket of trees, another 600 yards or so away. To his right, a flat field covered in a thick layer of fog that was slowly rising. Reynolds was knee deep in a dense, white fog that clung to the damp earth. True to his training, today was not his day to die.

Striding across the grass, Reynolds held his rifle at the ready, ammo slung across his shoulders and pistols in his belt. His heart pounded against his chest.

He heard the damp padding of feet on wet grass coming up behind him. Spinning around, Reynolds tried to make out what it was through the fog. He could see something coming toward him, rippling through the white fog that clung low to the ground. The head of a man rose up out of the swirling cloud of white. Reynold's stomach dropped. In place of eyes were dark, empty sockets.

For a moment, Reynolds stood frozen. The anatomy was becoming clearer: one quarter naked man, three quarters dog. The creature scrambled across the ground, toward Reynolds, baring its teeth.

In a rush of adrenaline, Reynolds raised his weapon and fired. The sound of the shot was dampened by the fog. The man-dog snarled and lurched backward as blood squirted from its human shoulder. Reynolds fired again, and this time his mark was true. The shot blasted straight through the cranium, which exploded in a fountain of red, and the creature collapsed.

Breathing heavily, Reynolds turned and began to walk briskly toward the house. He saw movement through the fog to his left, something coming from the grove of trees. Reynolds raised his rifle, took aim at what he thought was the head, and fired. He heard a muffled thud and saw a shape collapse.

Reynolds was almost to the front porch when the door burst open and foot soldiers in helmets began to pour out, all armed.

Five were through the door in a neat and tidy line, as if they were in a ballet performance. Their heads swiveled simultaneously to stare straight at Reynolds as they raised their weapons.

Reynolds did not give them a chance. With one blast, he blew the faces off the first two soldiers in line. Their helmets went flying, putrid juices raining down. Other shots rang out from behind the house.

Striding forward, Reynolds gave the third soldier a kick in the gut. The soldier fell backward into his comrades, and Reynolds saw another pair of empty, eyeless sockets, which he also blasted to oblivion.

The doorway was blocked by a heap of corpses and two struggling, eyeless monsters. Cursing, Reynolds reached down and collected a loaded revolver on the ground before putting the creatures out of their misery. He slung the rifle over his shoulder, and pulled out his two pistols, gripping one in each hand.

Reynolds stepped over the mound of bodies, and entered the house. A figure lunged at him, arms outstretched. Reynolds raised the pistol and fired at the head. Liquid sprayed everywhere, and the body dropped to the ground.

As he turned a corner into the main hall, a volley of bullets made him duck down and step back. There were at least twenty on the stairway leading to the second floor.

Bullets rained down as Reynolds took cover behind a solid wall. He looked for something, anything, to throw. There was a crystal vase on a piece of furniture behind him, along with two chairs. Reynolds reached for the vase, thought better of it, and grabbed a chair instead. With a grunt, he launched it across the hall to the other side of the room.

Sure enough, the gunfire followed the arc of the chair.

Just enough time for me to pop one in the head.

Reynolds aimed his pistols around the corner and fired. One, two, three, four. Each head exploded like a melon. But he had drawn the gunfire back. And there were sodden footfalls on the stairs.

He did not even consider stopping. Reynolds charged forward, aiming and firing at every head. They burst, and their bodies fell to the ground. From upstairs, a maniacal laugh peeled out, loud enough to be heard over the shooting. Reynolds dove at the feet of an approaching soldier. Knocking the soldier's feet out from under him, Reynolds avoided instant death. The soldier took a bullet for him but continued to move in the most life-like fashion. Reynolds struggled as the soldier's body pressed down upon him, drenching him in putrid fluids. A woman's voice cried out, and from under the soldier's arm, Reynolds saw an old man on the stairs fighting soldiers with a wooden staff.

With a grunt, Reynolds rolled. Pulling the broken soldier over him, he squatted and stood up. Another shot fired and landed in the soldier's back. Reynolds crouched forward and ran for the staircase. Reaching the first landing, Reynolds moved to discard the soldier. To his dismay, two strong hands clasped his neck tightly, groping at his throat.

Reynolds leaned to the left and ducked his head and shoulders to the right. Reynolds tumbled to the floor. Ducking and rolling, he took shelter behind an overturned table, and moved fast to reload his weapons.

CHAPTER 19

Shattering Convention a Second Time

Inara stood before the three panes of glass, each with a different version of herself. In her hand she held the stone the mysterious Dondio had given her. *Say these words,* Dondio had told her. *And hold on tight. Let the mirror's magic do the rest.*

"It seems my influence has left you," Malocchio said from behind her. "Shame, that. You were becoming such a cold killer. Pitting men against each other in your dungeons? An entertaining idea. I aim to try it one day."

Inara turned to see him. There were footsteps and fighting in the hall.

"You won't have the chance, I'm afraid."

Malocchio smiled. He was a handsome man, tall, with features cut from stone. His hair was as black as hers, with a widow's peak and sharply slanted eyebrows. He would have looked absurd in clothing that was too small, but the power that emanated from him overwhelmed any comical aspect of his appearance.

"Now, now," he said. "Your time of arrogance is finished. Now is your time to grovel. I can't kill you until you've properly groveled."

"You leave her be!" called out Ed, entering the room. He held a rifle leveled at Malocchio's back. It warmed Inara's heart to see American Edward, but she feared for him. She gripped the stone more tightly.

Malocchio sighed. "I'll have time for you soon, Gael. Just please try and keep yourself alive until then." With a swish of his hand, Ed was knocked back out of the open door, and it slammed shut. Immediately, Ed could be heard smashing into the door, calling after Inara. Malocchio laughed.

"Your Gael is brave but stupid. One moment he's bashing in your brains, the next he's risking all to save you. Why do all Gaels remind me of Artur?"

"You've lived too long," Inara said. "All you do is reminisce."

"And all you do is dream," Malocchio replied, stepping closer. Ed was still trying to knock down the door. "You dreamed of freedom from the Strega cycle, you dreamed of freedom from me, your proper lord and master. I wager you've dreamed that the gods would see your struggle and send an agent to save you. But you've always known, ever since your mother was slain, that you were on borrowed time." Malocchio was within arm's reach of her now. "You cannot attack me with my own power." His hand stretched out, gliding over her chest and up to her throat. They were big hands, enough to wrap around the whole of her neck. "You are a helpless little girl again, shivering and powerless with a dry cunt and without a clue how to survive. I shall not teach you survival. I will teach you how to die. You'll get a death for each one of mine. For each of my torments." As Malocchio squeezed her throat, he drew his other hand up to her face, hovering over her eyes.

The door shook as shards of wood fell from it. Ed was still screaming, still pounding his way inside. Inara smiled at the demon.

"One death was more than enough for me, thank you," she said. Then she spoke the words Dondio taught her. "*Fluisca il sangue del nemico. Illumina la pietra dell'eternità.*"

Malocchio's eyes shot open wide. She turned to the mirror and hurled the empty moonstone at the center pane of glass. It shattered on impact, but the broken glass did not scatter on the floor. The shards collapsed inward, and a great wind roared through the parlor. The Strega's shelves, her trinkets, bowls and keepsakes all tumbled and burst into pieces as the whirlwind swept the room's contents through the air. Inara felt herself being pulled toward the mirror.

"No!" he wailed. His handsome face was twisted into a monstrous grimace, his eyes fire and his mouth a gash. "No! It can't be!"

Her dark hair whirled about her head, blinding her as they both tumbled to the floor and slid. Inara struggled to find a breath, and in the confusion and winds it took a moment before she realized that the pressure she felt was Malocchio's hands around her neck, strangling her. She did not try to fight back. If this was why the Strego Bianco brought her back, to do this one deed and trap Malocchio in the space between the worlds, then so be it.

"You're coming with me, bitch," Malocchio said through gritted teeth. They were almost to the mirror now, being pulled into the broken space like blood swirling down a drain. "You're going to be entwined with me forever. You're-"

The sharp end of a bayonet burst through the front of Malocchio's under-sized shirt. The demon tried to wail, but only managed to cough up blood. Ed was behind him, and he pulled the bayonet out and drove it into Malocchio's back again. And again. The demon's hands left Inara's throat, and she sucked in a painful breath, but a breath none the less.

Then Dondio was there too, his vest ragged and covered in blood, his staff much the same. The old man swung the staff, its solid bulbous end smacking into Malocchio's jaw with a crunch that knocked him off of Inara and a step closer to the mirror. All it took from there was Ed driving a shoulder forward and the demon tumbled right into the vortex. For a moment, Inara feared Malocchio might be strong enough. He held himself there before the opening, the muscles in his arms taut with strain. Inara suddenly realized why the mirror seemed so useless to her mother and to herself. It was a creation of the Streghi Bianchi, not of Streghe Nere. Had her mother known that?

Malocchio struggled, his teeth clenched, blood drawing off his skin in horizontal red lines. Malocchio's lip curled into a smile as if he knew he could beat the magic. He braced himself and leaned away from the mirror. But then silver vines broke from the border around the glass. The silver vines punched themselves into Malocchio's flesh. He screamed as the metal branches entwined him, digging under his flesh to wrap directly around his bones.

Like a great tentacled beast pulling a meal into its gullet, the vines forced Malocchio through the frame, inside of the mirror. The silver vines slid past one another as they wove a screen over the open pane. The screams of Malocchio silenced and the air became still. The silver vine leaves twinkled innocently replacing the gaping hole through which Malocchio had passed.

Ed was on a knee next to Inara as she coughed. He took her hand, apologizing again and again, but she barely heard. Inara was free. The taint of Malocchio was gone, like the clouds parting after the rainy-season. Dondio leaned on his staff, smiling down at them. Why did this strange Strego Bianco seem so familiar?

"Who are you?" Inara asked him, once she could speak. She had asked the man this once already, and he had avoided the question. "Why did you come here?" Ed looked up at the Strego as well, seeming to want answers himself.

Dondio shrugged. "I am a priest," he offered, and added with a fatherly smile, "I am here at the behest of the Lady of Life."

"We'll have time enough to make acquaintances," Ed said. "Let us get out of this place."

"No, we will not," Dondio said sadly, his smile faltering. "This is a dangerous land for the both of you. That you have found each other is rare."

"I have an army base not far from here," Ed urged. "We can all—"

"No, we cannot," Dondio interrupted. "You both must go now. You must bring *La Religione Vecchia in un altro mondo...* to a new world." He gave Inara one final smile before he said his fateful words.

> *Possa il tuo scopo essere chiaro.*
> *Possa la tua strada essere ben illuminata.*
> *Possa il tuo cuore brillare di luce tra le ombre.*
> *Fluisca il sangue delle cuore,*
> *Fluisca il sangue delle cuore,*
> *Fluisca il sangue del nemico.*
> *Illumina il percorso per un altro mondo.*

Then he threw another stone at the mirror.

"You bastard!" Ed yelled. A pane shattered and the winds picked up again. The silver vines once more began to move.

"Plant your roots somewhere," Dondio called after them. "And find life anew."

Inara was lifted. She felt Ed's arms tighten around her waist as they plummeted through the mirror, toward the strange light of another world.

CHAPTER 20

Sunrise

Dondio padded his way out of the house, stepping over the corpses lining the stairs. There would be many questions when the Americans arrived. In his pocket he carried matches, which he lit and dropped. He hoped his daughter and Edward would find happiness somewhere safe. They would find a world that did not yet know the teachings of The Lady of Life, and Inara could make her atonement by spreading *La Religione Vecchia*. He lit another match and dropped it on the fine Persian rug. An old man could dream.

His power spent, Dondio thought he might walk for a bit. He could no longer summon his filly, but that was no matter. He felt good. He had accomplished so much. Before leaving, he dropped a few more matches on the stairs, in the kitchen, in the hall. When he saw an oil lamp he knocked it over. The entire place would be consumed by flames

147

soon. By the gods, he wished he could have gone through the mirror with them. But no, the Lady would have told him if that was what she wanted. It seemed that he was destined to walk this earth forever.

Dondio walked out into the fresh light of dawn, the eastern sun feeling warm against his flesh. It was bright and made him blink. He never saw the soldier raise his rifle and fire. Dondio's last thought before the bullet went through his brain was that it was the most gorgeous sunrise he had ever seen.

~~~

A FIST MADE of guilt socked Reynolds in the gut. He had thought the scrawny hermit was a soldier at first. Reynolds' nerves must have been more tense than he realized. The white-beard was filthy and covered with blood, and Reynolds had fired when he registered the person was not one of his men. He was immediately sorry. It was a clean shot. At least the hermit did not suffer, but it seemed like a true shame.

The sergeant sighed and looked up to the sky, as if to ask for help. That is when he saw the smoke. Now he smelled it, too. Reynolds bounded up the porch to the front door and peered in. The place was catching fire. He saw the curtains burning, paint on the nearby wall bubbling, smoke filling the rooms. The house was lost, and if he went back inside, he would be as well.

Reynolds leapt off the front porch and ran back toward the road. "Sorry, old timer," Reynolds said as he passed hermit's corpse.

As the house burned, the fog lifted.

~~~

"THERE HE IS," the woman's voice said.

Arnold gasped when he saw the priest, dead with a bullet hole through the forehead. The house was heavily ablaze with fire. Dark smoke billowed from the windows. Urgently, he grasped the priest under the arms and began to pull.

"Do you have it?" The woman's voice echoed in his head.

"Yes," Arnold said, surprised to find the stone still clutched in his left hand.

"You can do this," she urged. Her voice was comforting, like familiar music.

"I'm not sure," he mumbled.

"You can do this," she said. "The Lady of Life has shown faith in you, Samson Arnold. Have faith in yourself."

Arnold's back straightened and he nodded resolutely.

The sound of approaching army trucks rumbled as Arnold pulled the priest's body into the protective cover of trees. In the distance, the house was a towering pillar of flame. Crouching over Dondio's body, Arnold folded the stone in the priest's hand and began to say the words.

Dear Reader, what did you think?
Your unbiased thoughts and feedback are welcome in this creative
landscape! You are invited to share your unbiased opinion.

Please go to ByNicholasAnthony.com and Share a Review.